Midsummer Eve. That was a constant in all the stories about The House, as if it magically appeared on that single night.

The first time Holy Joe told her about the house, Francesca ignored him. She ignored him the second and third and fourth times as well, but despite her efforts, the house was getting under her skin. She started to dream about it.

And she started collecting the stories.

As soon as she started listening, she realized that everyone in her neighborhood talked about it. The House, they called it, the capital letters obvious in their tone.

Most of the stories, a jumble of rumors, drunken ramblings and wishful thinking, were nowhere as clear—or as obvious—as that single reference to the house appearing on Midsummer Eve.

One year, from one Midsummer Eve to the following—that's what people said about the people who had disappeared for a year and come back more than just rested. They came back transformed.

Kate Austin

Kate Austin has worked as a legal assistant, a commercial fisher, a brewery manager, a teacher, a technical writer and a herring popper. Go ahead—ask her anything. If she doesn't know the answer, she'll make it up, because she's been reading and writing fiction for as long as she can remember.

She blames her mother and two grandmothers for her reading and writing obsession—all of them were avid readers and they passed the books and the obsession on to her. She lives in Vancouver, Canada, where she can walk on the beach whenever necessary, even in the rain.

She'd be delighted to hear from readers through her Web site, www.kateaustin.ca.

KATE AUSTIN

Awakening

AWAKENING

isbn-13:9780373881024

isbn-10: 0373881029

This edition published by arrangement with Harlequin Books S.A.

TheNextNovel.com

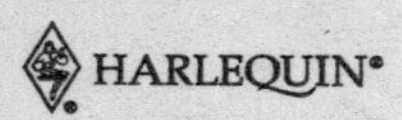

PRINTED IN U.S.A.

From the Author

Dear Reader,

This book was born on a rainy and cold Valentine's night. My friend Patrick and I had been to the theater (I have no idea what we saw, although looking back, it probably should have been *A Midsummer Night's Dream*) and on the way home we passed a downtown alley lit up by neon. That image—and the conversation we had about it—stuck in my head. The alley waited for several years before Francesca arrived to bring it to life.

I loved writing *Awakening* because of the characters, but also because of the setting. There is something about Mystic Hearts—the Victorian candy store, the English country garden surrounding it—that speaks to me at a very deep level. I live in a green and verdant land, but England, as it does for many of us, feels like my second home.

I hope you enjoy *Awakening*. Please e-mail me at kate@kateaustin.ca or check out my Web site, www.kateaustin.ca, for more information and contests with exciting prizes. If you'd prefer to send me a letter, my address is P.O. Box 73523, Downtown RPO, Vancouver, BC, V6E 1T9, Canada.

Kate

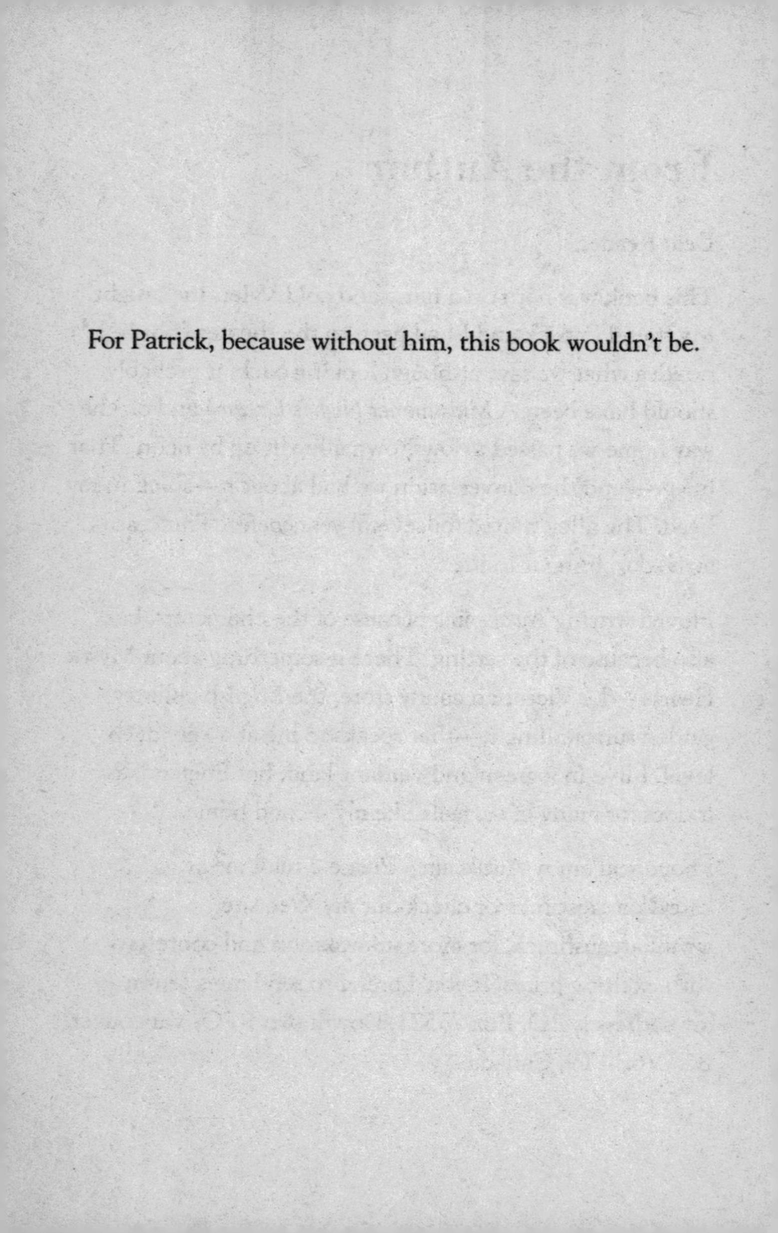

For Patrick, because without him, this book wouldn't be.

CHAPTER 1

I know a bank where the wild thyme blows,
Where oxlips and the nodding violet grows,
Quite over-canopied with luscious woodbine,
With sweet musk-roses and eglantine.
—Shakespeare, *A Midsummer Night's Dream*

Midsummer eve, 10:00 p.m.

Francesca couldn't help herself. She stood at the window of the Internet café, the Mouse and Icon, and spoke to the fogged-up glass.

"It was a dark and stormy night."

Her mind moved in clichés when she was tired, which was more often than not. This job, number two, meant five nights a week at this café and three nights out of those five came on the heels of a long shift at a coffee shop down the street.

Clichés were a very bad sign, especially this early in her week.

The mostly muted din of the twenty computers, four printers, three pinball machines and their accompanying humans, had turned into an all-out roar this midsummer evening. She checked the room again. Every keyboard clicked, every printer whirred.

And the pinball machines? They rattled and boinged and pinged. And voices occasionally screamed, "*Yes*" as an accompaniment to all the other noises.

She strolled as casually as she could manage through the rows of faded office chairs. The chairs weren't occupied by the usual crowd of university students and kids from the many ESL schools in the neighborhood. At least half of the chairs held women, which was unusual in itself, but these women were her age, which was so odd as to shift it over from unusual to downright peculiar.

Francesca spent most of her nights surrounded by young men so engrossed in their computer screens that they barely acknowledged her existence as she passed behind them.

Francesca smiled.

She liked this job.

Liked it despite the fact that most of her customers didn't remember to shower most days. Neo, the owner of the Mouse and Icon, had bought the most expensive systems on the market and he upgraded them every three months. The Mouse had equipment even hackers envied.

Francesca spent a fair amount of time trying not to think about where Neo found the money because he certainly didn't make it at the Mouse and Icon.

But because of it, even serious users whose apartments were full of computer equipment dropped in once or twice a week. Serious users, like all addicts, didn't have much time for personal hygiene.

The regulars stopped at the front desk to pay their tab and sometimes to decompress on their way home, their eyes glazed from staring at the screen. They told her about their projects, their childhoods, their dreams—they talked as a way to come down from the Internet buzz and get ready for a few hours sleep before they got up for school in the morning.

Sometimes, when it was very late and the streets were quiet, when only one or two tired boys sat at the computers in the back, when the Mouse's buzz had turned still, Holy Joe, one of the most regular of the regulars, would stop by the desk on his way home to talk about the house.

"It's there," he'd say, "I know it is. Father Henry used to talk about it."

"But where?" Francesca would always ask, wanting to believe but scared to.

"I don't know. But Father Henry isn't the only one who's been there. You know that big cop who works at the station down the street? The one who runs the children's fund?"

"Yes," she'd say. "He's always smiling." Something she noticed because it was so unusual in this neighborhood. The father and the cop. Their smiles, so sweet and serene, made Francesca want to believe.

After those conversations she'd spend the rest of the night weaving together the few snippets she'd heard, daydreaming herself into the safety of the house. Another world.

Francesca knew not just anyone could get there. She knew that, even though it was near, it wasn't really here. Basically, she thought, she knew… nothing about the house.

Eventually, she'd throw up her hands in disgust and resolve to live in *this* world, *this* place. It was hard enough to cope without dreaming about some stupid otherworldly mirage.

She pulled herself back into the Mouse and Icon, home of supercharged and faintly smelly young men.

But tonight? Tonight the pungent aroma of male sweat and unwashed hair had been tempered by the sweeter scents of fruit shampoos and floral perfumes.

Francesca scanned the room. The regulars huddled together in the back, more comfortable in the shadows, while the women occupied the stations closest to the windows and the desk.

Francesca might have been one of them if she'd had money, with their careful haircuts and discreet makeup. Women of a certain age, fighting off middle-aged bulges, making the best of their singleness. Taking classes, exercising, eating out and vacationing with friends, working at jobs that paid enough....

Her mental record skipped at that thought. She worked at two jobs and even together they didn't pay enough for luxuries like vacations and fancy restaurants. Sometimes they barely paid enough for food and rent.

She watched the room's reflection in the window and wondered about the women. She knew why they were here, for the same reason she hadn't hesitated about taking this extra shift. There was something about Midsummer eve that inspired longing.

Shakespeare had it right—that whirlwind night of transformation and longing and foolishness. Francesca could see some of that happening right here at the Mouse.

She wondered what kinds of chat rooms they were surfing so diligently. Francesca had spent her share of nights surfing the Net, checking into chat rooms and reading blogs, but she'd given it up. It had just made her feel more isolated.

She turned her back to the room and stared out at the rain. Francesca mostly tried to ignore the solitary state of her life, but having all these women here was bringing it all back to her.

It wasn't that she spent all that much time alone; she worked too many hours for that. She had the people she worked with, her regulars at the coffee shop, and she had—occasionally—Susannah and C.J.

But *alone* was the word she used to describe herself in those darkest hours of the night when she couldn't sleep. When she lay in bed, tossing and turning, unable to get comfortable because her body was reacting to the chanting of her restless mind:

Alone.

Alone.

Alone.

And she didn't seem to be able to do anything about that. She loved the time she spent with Susannah and C.J., either separately or together, but they were busy, both of them, and so was she.

Anyone who worked two full-time jobs didn't have much time for socializing. Add exhaustion to that, and Francesca didn't get out much.

Francesca was used to solitude. She'd basically

been alone since her mother had moved to Italy just after Francesca's sixteenth birthday. Her father had died years earlier.

The first five years after moving out on her own had been tough, more than tough, but Francesca had motored through them, always earning sufficient money to pay the rent and buy enough groceries to survive. She grinned at the thought of the tons of mac and cheese she'd eaten in those years.

It was a wonder that her skin hadn't turned pale orange. And she still kept a few boxes in her cupboard, not so much because she needed to save money, but because it was comfort food for her. If she had a supremely bad day, she made mac and cheese. If she was too tired to cook, she made mac and cheese.

She didn't eat it as much as she had even a couple of years ago, but that had more to do with her tastes than her need for it. Even so, she always replaced the box immediately after she'd consumed its contents.

Because food was a safety thing for Francesca. She'd spent too many years living on the edge, so her cupboards and her fridge were full. Always. She had cans of soup and tomato sauce and tuna. She even had cans of salmon—although she bought them on sale—piled high in the back. She had bags of pasta and extra cereal.

She bought food on sale, even food she didn't normally eat. She took advantage of two-for-one sales and had even, one year when she'd been slightly more flush than usual, bought a small secondhand freezer she kept stocked with meat and frozen vegetables.

Francesca loved coming home from a double shift, opening her cupboards and seeing all the cans in their neat stacks. She'd open the freezer and smile at the perfectly labeled meats and fish and vegetables. She'd open her refrigerator and admire the jars of jam and pickles, the bags of fresh fruit and vegetables, the cans of pop and juice.

For those few moments, she felt safe.

And that was what she wanted more than anything.

Because safety hadn't been a big part of her life so far. Francesca slept with a light on and a baseball bat on the pillow beside her. She had three locks on her door and bars on her windows.

Nothing had ever happened to her, nothing more than was to be expected living in a part of town that crawled with drug dealers and muggers and thugs. She wanted to move, who wouldn't? But she couldn't earn enough money to leave this neighborhood.

And it was familiar. Not safe, but known. She knew what to expect when she walked down the street, knew who to avoid and what doors opened to sanctuary. Would she be safer somewhere else? Maybe. Maybe not.

She'd been stalked, she thought with a shiver, but she'd always managed to get home or to the coffee shop or the Mouse before the footsteps had caught up to her.

After the first time, she began to carry a can of pepper spray and a flashlight. Francesca's work schedule wasn't conducive to walking home in the safe hours when the sun shone and the buses ran. And she couldn't afford cab fare.

But Francesca considered her life a pretty good one. She didn't have a lot of money but she had food and shelter, and a lot of the people she saw every day didn't have either. She had two good jobs and she made enough money to get by. Just.

That mattered. Getting by. Making it through the day, through the week, through the month. And she managed that.

And she had more fun than anyone could have expected watching her life from the outside.

Francesca's motto was Life Wasn't Meant to Be Easy, But It Was Meant to Be Fun. She lived by it. She watched for fun, coaxed it to her, especially the kind of fun she could watch from the sidelines—other people's stories, mostly.

So she watched for the funny, the odd, the unusual. She cultivated it.

Francesca was pretty sure that her life was going as well as could be expected under the circumstances. She had nothing to complain about.

She just wished she could get rid of the fear that she felt every single day, that big black hole in the pit of her stomach that writhed when she had to leave the coffee shop or the Mouse and Icon to walk home in the dark.

CHAPTER 2

Neo should have been at the Mouse and Icon by now, but he'd called to ask her to stay an extra hour. He had a date.

And because that was so unusual—both the asking and the date—Francesca had agreed to stay until midnight. She was regretting it now.

All the women had left just after ten, as if their computers had succumbed to a virus that printed a message on their screens saying *Go home now*. The few addicts, still ensconced in their dark little group at the back of the café, were as silent as it was possible to be in a room filled with computers.

Francesca listened to the background hum of the machines, the light tip-tapping of fingers on the keyboards, the even fainter wisps of breath, in and out and in.

She didn't like being here tonight.

Her favorites—Holy Joe, Frank and Harold—hadn't come in this evening. She counted on them to keep an eye on her, even while they were immersed in their computer games. The Mouse and Icon was their home away from home and they treated her as their surrogate big sister.

They were here almost every night but not one of them had shown up. They couldn't all have dates, could they? Nah. Francesca shook her head. That would require three miracles, something almost impossible to contemplate.

She made a mental note to take a deep breath the next time she saw the gamers. If they'd showered recently, they'd had dates. She grinned. She could hardly wait to hear about their exploits, those stories were sure to entertain her.

But for now, she felt alone. And frightened.

She felt a hint of terror traveling up her spine. She peered out the window at the rain, then back into the gloom at the rear of the Mouse.

Her watch said 10:45. Maybe Neo would be early. She tallied the register, put the tally sheet in the drawer and locked it. Not much cash tonight. All the women had paid with credit or bank cards. Like her, though for different reasons, they didn't carry much money.

The door swung open, bringing with it the chill dampness of the storm.

"Neo."

"Hey, babe."

He sauntered in, looking smug, his arm around a young woman wrapped in his tan trench coat.

"This is Tracy. Tracy, this is Francesca."

Tracy looked at her with a hint of disdain. Francesca hid her smile. She knew exactly what the girl was thinking.

Is she competition?

Francesca concentrated on appearing innocuous and friendly, but not too friendly. It worked. Tracy smiled and sat down at the chair in front of the desk, showing the skimpy outfit beneath the coat.

Neo did a quick scan of the room.

"Quiet night?"

"Nope," Francesca said. "Weird night. All women until forty-five minutes ago and then they all disappeared. And Holy Joe and crew didn't show their faces at all."

Neo's eyes flickered in disbelief.

"None of them?"

"Not one."

He shrugged his shoulders.

"No point in worrying about it now. Go on home, Francesca, I'll see you tomorrow night."

Francesca's heart pounded at the thought of stepping out the front door, but she was not going to show fear. No way. Neo might offer her a ride home and she'd have a hard time saying no.

She wasn't sure why the fear was so strong tonight; there was no real reason for it. At least no reason she could see.

She took another look at the street. Empty. Empty streets didn't scare her.

She took a deep breath. Rain. Wet pavement. Muggy summer night. No smoke, no sweat, no cheap cologne. It smelled fine.

She stepped farther onto the sidewalk and listened. Nothing out of the ordinary. Rain hitting the pavement. The faint hiss of transformers. Tires on the damp pavement on the next street over.

Francesca scolded her inner self.

"Nothing," she whispered, "nothing to be scared of. Come on, you big baby, let's go home."

She girded her loins. Francesca grinned at the cliché. She'd been reading way too much fantasy in the past couple of months.

"Step," she said. "Right."

She placed her right foot carefully on the sidewalk. "Left." Followed it with her left.

The routine got her going, kept her going for the fifteen minutes it took to get down the block, around a couple of corners, and almost home, without seeing a single person. Unusual, but not unheard of.

She stopped at the corner of her block. Shadows, moving ones, in front of her building. She assessed the situation.

11:15. Not too late. And she had her keys ready and pepper spray in her hand.

"Go," she said out loud, "you'll be fine."

Francesca wasn't sure about that last part, but the fear that had her sweating now had been haunting her all night. Really, she thought, it had been haunting her for decades, some days worse than others.

This day had been a bad one. The trouble was how that totally uncalled for fear colored her thinking; sometimes she couldn't tell if the fear was legitimate or simply an extension of an already bad day.

She chose to believe it was the latter and strode towards her building, forcing confidence into her shoulders, her legs and her face. She relaxed her hands, holding the keys and pepper spray with something less than the death grip she'd used until now.

Three men stood at her front door. *Familiar*, Francesca thought with relief, *they belong*. Her fear level abated.

She was wrong.

She ran.

CHAPTER 3

Midsummer eve, midnight

Rain. And flashing neon turning the dark alley crimson. The illumination transformed the heavy drops into streams of bright red light.

Francesca couldn't read the sign producing the light, but she felt safer knowing something, someone, was at the end of the dark space. She ran faster, then faster again.

There was no one behind her, she was pretty sure of that, but her heart and lungs and legs disagreed. They urged her on, heart pounding, lungs gasping for air. And her legs wouldn't stop even though they ached and each step she took increased the pressure on her shins.

She'd had no exercise for months except the hours she spent on her feet at work, and she was so out of shape she could barely breathe. But lack of oxygen didn't stop her, nor the pain in her shins, nor her headache. She kept on running because now, for the first time, well, for the first time in forever, she had a goal. To reach the source of the neon flashes.

"I'm alive," she said, right out loud. And then she said it again. Even louder.

"I'm alive."

An hour ago she wouldn't have bet on that. The words hurt her ears but the sentiment buoyed her spirits. She would have time to experience the world again. She would enjoy the sights and sounds and smells.

She stopped for a moment to listen, to sniff the air for signs she wasn't sure she'd recognize.

She heard nothing except the rhythmic beat of the rain and, somewhere beyond human hearing, so faint she wasn't sure it was real, the sound of neon hissing. Maybe her imagination was working overtime, and then she wondered for a moment if it was the same sound as the northern lights—that faint hissing that accompanied the waves of color in the northern sky.

Suddenly, she wanted to be somewhere dark and cold and still. A place where the northern lights were visible. She wanted to see the sky blooming overhead and hear the sound of ether in the air.

She hated summer in this place. The air grew

thick and so dirty she could feel the brown sludge coating her throat and lungs.

She longed for the cool summer rain of the rain forest but she couldn't, wouldn't go back. Francesca never went back. The only way to cope with her fear was to run away from it. That's why she moved two or three times a year.

Another sound, a light skittering in the darkness. Rats didn't bother her. Not anymore. She'd lived in neighborhoods where four-legged rats had been the least of her worries.

And she smelled something...what? She thought about it for a moment. Oil. She looked down and saw the patterns in the shallow pools, undulating with the weight of the rain and the wind.

And smoke. She looked around, disbelief in her gaze. Nothing could burn in this rain. But she'd seen a program about spontaneous combustion once, late at night when the city slowed to a standstill and the oddest shows were the norm. Spontaneous combustion could strike the human body in the middle of a swimming pool. Okay, she thought, maybe that, but no other fire could flourish in this storm.

But Francesca had learned to be careful, to take no chances. She'd relearned that lesson with a vengeance tonight. She moved quietly to the center of the alley and tried to focus. She turned in a circle, taking deep breaths and looking first down, then up. People always forgot to look up. She'd had that lesson, along with many others, drilled into her by C.J. Self-defense for dummies, he called it. Francesca peered into the darkness.

She wasn't sure she would notice anything out of place but she did it anyway. "Follow procedure," she whispered, "even if it seems ridiculous under the circumstances."

C.J. had made it clear that there were no exceptions to that rule.

She looked for signs. There were no flickering red flames, no obvious fire, and the smell of smoke was gone. There was only the neon. Still flashing. She wanted to run toward it.

Silent now, she forced herself to stand in the exact center of the alley and tried to retrieve the skills she'd learned, the ones she'd abandoned along with too many other things. She knew the skills were there; they'd been drilled into her so deeply that they had to be, but they were elusive, hidden somewhere.

Wait. There was something else, something invading her nasal passages with an odor she wished she could forget. She couldn't. It would follow her wherever she went.

She wrinkled her nose, remembering the year she'd worked in the meat-packing plant. She'd spent the entire year taking three or four showers a day and never getting the smell of blood off her skin.

She tried to shut out the dense red smell clogging her nostrils. It might mean nothing. A dead animal, the back door to a butcher shop. She might even be imagining it.

That smell, and the nasty supervisor who went along with it, had convinced her to leave her small hometown and move to this city in the Midwest. Most times, now, she regretted that decision. Especially in the summer.

She moved on, farther into the alley, closer to the still unreadable flashing neon. Francesca no longer cared. In this neighborhood it might be anything from a tattoo parlor to an upscale nightclub. Whatever it was, she was going there.

She tucked her nose into the collar of her jacket, muffling the alley's odors, and ran. One foot in front of the other, each step jolting her spine and her shins and her head.

The headache was getting worse. Francesca grimaced. It would be a long while before it got better; she'd been awake for too long for anything to fix it but sleep.

And that was the one thing she wouldn't get—not in this lifetime, she thought. She wanted, desperately, a solid ten hours sleep without noises keeping her awake, without an alarm clock waking her far too early, without fretting in the middle of the night about finding the money to pay the bills.

Francesca put that thought away and continued toward the neon. There was nothing to be done about the headache, not now. The real pain would kick in soon enough but she had a few hours before she'd have to deal with the worst of it.

Perhaps by then she'd be safe.

Francesca felt the ache in her eyes. She blinked. It had been a long time since her eyes had watered over anything except onions.

Life got complicated when you allowed it to affect you. Francesca walked through life one foot in front of the other, avoiding emotional entanglements. She had enough to do just to pay the rent on her tiny room and to buy groceries for her hot plate.

She blinked again and shook herself all over, like Sandy, the golden Lab Susannah had babysat the summer they'd been twelve. Francesca thought about Sandy....

"No," Francesca said. "No. It's not safe."

She shook herself again and forced herself to focus on each step, each breath a meditation.

Breathe.

"In."

Breathe.

"Out."

She concentrated ferociously, fighting each thought of her past life, sending it to some other place. She needed to be in this moment, watching, listening. Distractions might kill her. Or worse.

She stopped, the crimson flash coming faster now, as if the sign's motor had sped up to double time. Her headache began to throb in rhythm with it—flash, throb, flash, throb.

Francesca closed her eyes but the neon flashed right through her eyelids. Her throat convulsed, vomit rising to the back of her tongue. She swallowed, twice, and spit the taste of it out into the oily pools at her feet.

She knew her safety might be only temporary so she decided to make the best of it. She would enjoy this silent place unless… Unless she heard or saw something that meant she'd have to start running again. She leaned against a grubby brick wall and studied it.

Grit. Dirt. She rubbed her hands on the wall, enjoying the rough grains on her palms. Francesca looked down but saw only shadows. She wanted to see the discoloration of her hands, wanted more evidence of reality, even if it was grubby.

This wall was real. She could feel it on her hands, feel its strength and age through her palms. She rested her cheek on the rough brick and once again fought back the tears.

She had no time for crying, no time for contemplation. She needed to find somewhere safe and she needed to find it now. Just because she didn't hear footsteps didn't mean someone wasn't following her. In this neighborhood, danger was a given.

"Oh, God." Francesca leaned against the wall, suddenly weak with sorrow.

But she couldn't call anyone, not even Susannah. Francesca hadn't spoken to her in weeks. And Francesca didn't feel badly about that. Susannah would be back soon enough and then Francesca would feel...

She wouldn't feel safe. She wasn't sure she'd ever feel safe, but she'd have someone to talk to.

Her best friend. Tall where Francesca was short. Living on the right side of the tracks while Francesca lived way on the wrong side. Susannah had enough money to buy anything she wanted, while Francesca had trouble buying milk some days.

But Susannah had stuck with Francesca through

everything. They'd been best friends since they'd met running away from bullies in the fifth grade. And Susannah never questioned Francesca's choices. She worried about them, Francesca saw it in her eyes, but she never questioned them, not out loud. Not even when Francesca had left home the day she'd turned sixteen.

Susannah had taken her to the bank, withdrawn every penny from her college fund, and had handed it over to Francesca.

"Call me," she'd said. "Call me collect. I'll fix it with Mom. It'll be okay."

And Francesca had called her. Every Sunday forever, for as long as she could remember, she had called Susannah at nine o'clock, though never once, no matter that it meant pasta for dinner every night for a week, had she called collect.

"I'm not thinking about those days, not now. Maybe never. Being a teenager sucked." She turned toward the wall again and rested her forehead against it.

Francesca thought about the years when it had been just her and Mom. When she had waited each afternoon for her mother to come home from work and help her with her homework. She never did. Francesca's mother wasn't interested in her; she was interested in men.

That had been an easy lesson to learn after her dad had died. She'd been a good mother before that day, but after? Francesca's mother saw the world in order of men, then work, and then a very long way behind, Francesca.

It wasn't that she didn't love Francesca. She did. Even Francesca had to admit it when she remembered those nights when her mother had come in late and sat down on the bed next to her. She'd run her hand across Francesca's forehead and hummed. *Mama's gonna buy you a mockingbird, and if that mockingbird don't sing, Mama's gonna buy you a diamond ring.*

She never did buy Francesca a diamond ring, or anything else. They were both so lost.

Francesca found herself, for the first time in many years, remembering the day they'd lost themselves and each other.

Francesca remembered mostly being pissed off.

The sun had shone in an azure sky. The grass practically glowed and the cherry blossoms floated down to cover it like drifts of pink snow. The only thing out of place was the brown dirt waiting to be shoveled into the open grave.

She wanted rain and wind and black skies for this funeral. Needed them, really. To make this feel real to her. Her mother's quiet sobs weren't enough.

Francesca knew why she needed the rain and the clouds. Because somewhere deep inside, in a room with a big black door with a solid lock whose key was buried deep in the earth, she wanted to bury her love for her father along with his body. She wished the love away, but it wouldn't go.

Even now, decades later, Francesca sometimes had trouble believing he was dead. One day he was there, the next he was gone.

And then, years of hell later, just before her sixteenth birthday, Francesca's mother booked a trip to Italy.

"I need a break, darling," she said to Francesca. "And Susannah's mom is happy to have you for a few weeks."

She tousled her daughter's hair, even though Francesca had told her a million times not to do it.

"It'll be good for both of us," she said.

Francesca knew her mother meant that she couldn't cope with Francesca's sorrow any longer, not combined with her own. Neither could Francesca.

Her mother sent postcards to Francesca telling her how much she enjoyed Rome and Florence and Venice and how much she wished she was there. But she didn't. Not really. And Francesca wanted to ignore the grief her own way.

Late nights, loud music, lots of boys. Francesca wanted the waters of Lethe to wash over her and make her forget her father.

I'll be home soon, the postcards from her mother said, but she wasn't. She'd loved Bellagio, a narrow crescent of a town perched on the edge of Lake Como, and she'd settled there, always promising to come home but never quite making it. Francesca got postcards, the occasional short letter, and one phone call a year, on her birthday.

She supposed she was lucky that her mother even remembered her birthday. The odd thing was that she didn't really blame her mother. She understood her.

Both of them dealt with their grief by running away from home.

CHAPTER 4

Francesca forced herself to move away from the support of the wall. Time to find the source of the red flashes.

She took a step.

"Damn," Francesca whispered in a pained voice. "Damn. Damn. Damn."

She gingerly took another step and stopped dead in her tracks. Her feet, already turned to prunes, got wetter—if that was possible. The blisters she'd acquired during the race to get away had burst and now her socks were wet from both the inside and the outside.

Francesca wiggled her toes to check for the twenty-dollar bill in her right shoe. Yep, there it was. Right under the blisters. The thought of taking it out of her sock and using it made her queasy.

Keeping that twenty dollars in her shoe was something her mother had taught her when Francesca had first started going out on her own. She'd reinforced it when Francesca had begun dating.

"Take this twenty, sweetie," she'd say, offering up a brand-new twenty-dollar bill, "And tuck it into your sock. That way, no matter what happens, you can get home."

Francesca had wanted to refuse the money, but she hadn't. And she'd never forgotten the advice. Even after she'd moved away from home, and no matter how poor she was, she always kept a single twenty-dollar bill in her dresser drawer and tucked it into her shoe before she left home.

This night, Francesca thought, her mother might have saved her life. Or, if not her life, she'd saved her from pneumonia. She was going to spend that money on hot chocolate in a warm coffee shop somewhere. Even the worst neighborhoods had coffee shops.

Francesca learned early on that tucking the bill in her sock gave her blisters, but if she tucked it in exactly the right place between her sock and her shoe, just under her instep, she didn't even notice it was there.

She hadn't dated much, not once since she'd gotten out of the mess she'd made of her life after she'd left home. But dates or not, Francesca took that bill with her everywhere.

She hobbled down the alley, trying to stay out of the puddles, an impossible task in the dark. When she reached the end of the alley, she stood there with her mouth open, the hot sticky rain dripping down her face and turning cold on contact.

The yellow house with white shutters, highlighted by the flashing red neon, looked like a five-year-old wearing her mother's cocktail dress.

Francesca smiled, an odd little grimace composed equally of pain and surprise. The Victorian house shouldn't be on this street, she thought. It belonged in some small town lost in the mists of time, a place where children still played in the streets, where grandparents rocked on the front porch, where parents…

She stopped herself from going there and concentrated on the house in front of her.

The neon still flashed but now she could decipher it. It read Bains Candies.

A candy store? Francesca snorted. She knew what those words really meant. No *real* candy store would be in this neighborhood, nor open this late at night.

She checked again. Yep, the huge neon sign still flashed above the awning, and a miniature neon sign on the door said OPEN. It was too late for any legitimate candy store to be open.

"Damn," she whispered, a shiver of fear running through her veins.

Francesca watched the front window of the store. The inside was frosted over like her bathroom mirror after she'd had a hot shower. She saw a shadow pass behind the window but all she could tell for sure was that the shadow was probably human. She needed to get closer, to see who was inside.

But she didn't move. Her eyes drifted up the building and got stuck on the second floor. There were white lace curtains on the windows across the front. No lights in the rooms, but Francesca could imagine them.

The first time Holy Joe had told her about the house, Francesca had ignored him. She'd ignored him the second and third and fourth times as well, but despite her efforts, the house got under her skin. She'd started to dream about it.

And she'd started collecting the stories.

As soon as she'd started listening, she'd realized that everyone in her neighborhood talked about it, from teenagers to cops to the old guys who hung out in the coffee shop. The House, they called it, the capital letters obvious in their tone.

Sometimes the stories were told in late-night whispers in the Mouse, sometimes in loud obnoxious drunken slurs in the coffee shop. Occasionally, Francesca heard something worth remembering.

The coffee shop. Late. Dark and cold. And two old guys in the corner. Francesca had recognized them. One owned the cigar store at the corner, the other a small business of some kind on the second floor of a building down the street. She didn't know what kind of business it was; the gilded letters on the windows had faded into unreadable shadows.

She poured their second cups of coffee and sat down at the counter. She saw them reflected in the mirror over the cash register, their heads close together, their hands moving in the air between them.

"Jimmy's gone," the cigar man said, "ever since last summer."

"The solstice, right?" the businessman asked.

"I think so. Some people think he killed himself, jumped off the bridge and got carried off down the river, but…"

"He didn't leave a note?"

The cigar man shrugged and sipped his coffee. "No one found a note. And his frogs died."

The businessman placed his hands together and shook his head. "Jimmy loved those frogs. He'd never let them die. Wouldn't matter how desperate he was."

The conversation switched to football and Francesca switched off listening and switched on analysis.

Midsummer eve. That was a constant in all the stories about the House, as if it magically appeared on that single night.

The rest of the stories, a jumble of rumors, drunken ramblings and wishful thinking, were nowhere near as clear—or as obvious—as that single reference.

The two men stood.

"We'll see Jimmy back in a few months," the cigar man had said as he'd walked out into the night.

One year, from one Midsummer eve to the following, that's what people said about Father Henry and the big cop, what they'd say about Jimmy, whoever he was. They disappeared for a year and came back more than just rested. They came back transformed.

Francesca returned her thoughts to the house in front of her. The second floor would be bedrooms, she thought, small and cozy. The room in the middle would be the biggest, with flowered wallpaper and white wicker frames on the mirrors and old-fashioned gilt-framed paintings on the walls. The paintings would be of young girls playing hoops in a garden, or black dogs lying next to ginger kittens, or beautiful castles seen mistily across the purple heather.

The bed would be covered with a white chenille spread and plump feather pillows piled up all higgledy-piggledy. The pillowcases would be eyelet lace, yellowed and soft with age. A rag rug on each side of the bed, and books, lots of books, on the bedside table next to a reading lamp.

Francesca gave herself a moment to imagine those books. Gene Stratton-Porter. Charles Kingsley. Georgette Heyer and Agatha Christie. Happy endings, all of them. Books she'd read in her childhood. The books she'd read in her grandmother's basement.

She imagined the other bedrooms. They were under the eaves so the ceiling would be sloped, and she might be able to feel safe sleeping on a single bed underneath that slope. The ceiling would be only a couple of feet above her head, protecting her from the night.

The wallpaper would be the same, only in *her* room, the flowers would be yellow roses and lilacs. The books she'd imagined in the biggest bedroom were quickly transferred into what she'd already come to think of as her room.

She wanted the windows on the left of the house as she faced it. She wanted candles as well as a reading lamp. And she wanted an old sheepskin rug on the floor. A rocking chair, one that didn't squeak when she rocked it, on the other side of the room from the bed. The room was no more than eight feet by ten feet, so she would only have to take two steps from the rocking chair to the bed.

And there was a lock on the door. Only one key, and Francesca carried it in her pocket. And a dead bolt that only she could lock. From the inside.

The bathroom just off the room had creaky wooden floors, but they were warm. No shower, but the tub was big and deep and clean. Francesca loved the bathroom.

Francesca laughed when she finished imagining the bathroom. A house that old, in this neighborhood, would be lucky to have a single ratty bathroom. But since this was her imagination, she could have whatever she wanted.

Of everything she'd missed over the years, there were two things she wanted more than anything else. A beautiful room of her own, where the lock was strong and the door capable of withstanding any force. A room where she could lock everybody else out and she couldn't hear their footsteps in the corridor.

She had an apartment, but it was the safety she craved. The strong lock, the privacy. A room that could give her those things was at the top of the list. And a bath ran a very close second.

Baths were for people with way more money than her; showers were smaller. And cheaper.

Francesca had just wasted ten minutes in the rain imagining this house as sanctuary. And it wasn't. It wasn't *the House*. It couldn't be. She knew that. Francesca Bond had absolutely nothing in common with Father Henry or the cop.

They weren't scared, not of anything. They walked through her neighborhood without fear, with sweet, serene smiles on their faces. They talked to everyone. Francesca? She talked to no one on the street.

But her options were limited. She needed to get out of the rain and Bains Candies was the only place. At least it was the only place open—Francesca looked around at the blank metal doors backing onto the alley, each of them with a slot at eye level to identify the customers—where she might be welcomed.

The shivers came more and more quickly now. Her teeth ached from clenching them together and her headache had progressed from bearable to excruciating. The water ran down her back and her broken blisters sent shards of pain across her feet.

She needed to get inside.

Francesca wanted one quick glimpse of the shadow behind the window to decide whether or not the candy store was safe.

She wasn't sure what she'd do when she got inside. She had the twenty-dollar bill in her shoe. She didn't like the thought of putting her shoe back on once she'd taken it off to get the money, but maybe she could do it if she had a few minutes to rest. Maybe the candy store had coffee or hot chocolate and a couple of small tables.

She could sit down, have a cup of hot chocolate, and decide what to do. Maybe, she thought, it was open all night and she could wait there until the morning. Until the rain stopped and she had worked out a plan.

Because being safe wasn't a plan. It was only a prayer.

Plans had steps. Take step A, which led you to step B, and then step C, all the way to step Z. That's what Francesca needed.

And to work out that plan, she needed time. And warmth, food and aspirin.

With that thought, she abandoned any worries about Bains Candies and walked right up to the door and through it. Right into heaven.

It smelled like her childhood. Chocolate and coconut and vanilla. A faint hint of orange. Nuts roasting. Coffee brewing. Under it all, Francesca smelled the scent of clean.

She ignored her headache and savored the

room she'd arrived in. Clean, butter-yellow paint covered the walls. She was willing to bet it matched the outside.

She did a quick scan. Only her. Not even a clerk. But it didn't feel empty; it felt like home.

A glass case covered one wall and then turned and stretched across the front of the room. The amber lights strung from the ceiling reflected off the sparkling glass. The floor tiles were black and white and red, the red ones the same brilliant crimson as the neon.

And inside the glass cases? A riot of colors and shapes. Strings of licorice, all kinds, bowls of foil-wrapped candies, jelly beans, marzipan mice and ducks and pigs. Candies Francesca had never seen before and couldn't imagine how they'd feel or taste on her tongue. Surrounding all of that glory, dozens of types and shapes and colors of chocolate.

Francesca couldn't help herself. She walked up to the nearest case, leaned down and pressed her nose against it, just as she would have done as a child.

She breathed in the comforting scent of chocolate and vanilla. And she remembered.

Francesca had been four or five when her grandfather had decided she was finally old enough to be in the kitchen while he made candy.

"You need to be careful," he said, pulling tins from a cupboard high above Francesca's head. "Candy's finicky. And it's dangerous. When you cook it, it turns liquid, and if you spill it on yourself, it sticks. And it hurts like..." He hesitated. "Like heck."

Grandpa's candy was a family tradition. The process, for the whole family, was a sign that all was well. And it was done in the same order and in the same way time after time.

He started by pulling the old tins—and they really were made out of tin—from the cupboards and piling them symmetrically on the counter. Francesca was allowed to watch but not to touch.

He didn't let her help him pile the tins because they were all odd shapes and sizes and he was a persnickety man. They had to be perfect and, even as Francesca got older, she could never get them tidy enough for him.

Once the tins were in place, he went into his room and crouched down beside the dresser. He removed the recipes from their safe nest in the bottom drawer. They were written in spidery faded handwriting on yellowed sheets of paper, each one carefully tucked into a zipped-shut plastic bag.

He put the recipes back into new plastic bags as each type of candy was finished. When he opened them the following year, the recipes were as pristine as they had been all those years ago when he'd first received them.

The recipes had been handed down from his great-grandfather to his son and to his son and to Francesca's grandfather.

They had been Francesca's until she'd lost them in one of her many moves. But the tins and the memories remained.

CHAPTER 5

Joshua's grin might have split a lesser face in half. But on his face, it looked almost natural.

He was a big man, even at eighty. Oh, maybe he'd lost an inch or two, but that still left him well over six feet, and thin with it. His clothes hung on him the way they would on a coat hanger. Big-boned in an Eastern European kind of way, people always said, though if he had that blood, it was so far back he couldn't find it.

He watched her from the kitchen through the one-way mirror. She looked like a drowned kitten, her hair flat against her head and her skin dimpled with goose bumps. A bedraggled half-dead kitten. He grinned again.

The woman looked like a kitten who'd just escaped the burlap sack. Her wet face contained both joy and fear, though Joshua suspected that the fear outweighed the joy.

"Why am I not surprised?" he said to the woman standing behind him.

"Maybe because you were expecting her?" The woman's voice was gnarled and painful and it came out so quietly Joshua had to turn toward her to make it out.

He didn't want to stop watching the woman in the store but he needed to hear what Marta had to say. Her once-proud voice barely made it past her larynx, puffing out of her mouth one muted word at a time.

As she finished speaking, Joshua touched her shoulder to encourage her to continue. He had learned over the years that Marta responded to his touch in a way she didn't to his voice.

From the moment he'd first seen Marta, sitting at the exact same table as tonight's guest, Joshua had known. He'd worried. There were too many reasons why he should ignore the surge of passion he'd felt when he saw her.

Saving lost souls was his calling and Marta had been one of the most damaged. Would his love tip the scale the wrong way? Even worse, he was twenty years older than her and she'd be gone in a year.

They were always gone in a year. The house represented a world out of time, where healing was possible. Where people who needed help didn't have to ask for it; it just happened.

Joshua had had almost forty years to consider the mechanics of the thing but the best he'd been able to come up with to explain it was this: the house existed in a real world, one with phones and doctors and stores. As he saw it, there was nothing unusual about the house or the world it inhabited at all.

It sat in a beautiful neighborhood—he'd bought it because of that—but all around was chaos. It was as if the people on his street had banded together to build a fortress and by doing that they had somehow succeeded in building an invisible wall, as well.

The wall, the barrier between the neighborhood and chaos, was permeable but only one way. Just like a one-way mirror. You could leave but you couldn't enter.

Except on Midsummer eve. Everything changed. One minute he'd be looking out his window at the garden sparkling in the sunlight, and the next? He'd be looking out at some dark alley (he was never sure if it was the same alley from year to year) and waiting for the front door to open on some lost soul.

And next year, at exactly the same time, the same thing would happen.

Sometimes the lost soul, once found, would stay in the neighborhood, but more often than not, they returned to their old lives. Only one had ever stayed in the house past their year's ending.

He smiled and reached for her hand, remembering the day she was supposed to have left.

"Joshua," Marta had whispered all those years ago. "I'm not leaving."

"Yes, you are," he said. "It's time. You've got to get on with your life."

He had spent most of his life saving people, and now he couldn't save himself. The pain was almost unbearable. The crack in his heart spread as if it were glass breaking in a shatter-proof window. One tiny crack, zipping from one side of his heart to the other, layering waves of pain with it, until he cried out.

Marta never wasted words when touch would do. She knelt on the bed beside him and then laid down, stretching herself to fit against his back. Her arms came around him and her face nestled into his neck.

She laughed. He tried to imagine her once-sweet voice tinkling with laughter. Now that laughter sounded painful passing through her throat, as if it were rocks being forced through a narrow channel.

He felt the laughter in her throat and her grin against his temple.

"Joshua, you know I am not leaving you. Not

now. Not ever. This healing—" she waved her hand across both their bodies "—this healing was for both of us. We will do this work together from now on."

And they had.

Each year on this night someone arrived in the store. Someone full of anguish and sorrow, someone in need of rescue.

It was seldom a simple rescue and Joshua believed that to be the reason it only happened once a year. Even with Marta's help, the cure took time.

Joshua had wondered, over the years, how the guests were chosen. He wondered what drew them to the house on this particular night, what the house saw in that person, and not in the thousands of others who needed help.

He knew there were no answers to those questions although he couldn't stop asking them. He asked them of Marta, still did, twenty years later. She simply got exasperated.

"It doesn't matter, does it? The people who need us arrive and we help them."

"Not us," Joshua said, waving his arm at the house around them. "Mystic Hearts helps them."

CHAPTER 6

"Whoa," Francesca whispered, leaning hard against the cool dampness of the glass. "No, not now. Don't do this. Please not now."

But her body didn't listen.

Handprints appeared on the glass as she slid to the floor and landed with her cheek resting against a black square. All she could see was black out of the corner of her right eye and a white square with her left.

And she couldn't move. She lay without even strength to raise herself up to her knees. C.J. would not be impressed. He'd spent years teaching her to marshal her strength no matter what happened; years working her until she swore she couldn't move and then making her rise above the pain.

"Enough," she'd cry, and he'd sweep her feet from beneath her yet again. She'd crash to the mat, slamming her head against the rubber, and he'd wait, his left foot tapping impatiently, while she crawled her way to her hands and knees.

Then he'd start again, leaning against her shoulders and tumbling her to the ground. He wouldn't stop. She'd sob, and he'd drop her again. She'd scream, and he'd throw her over his hip.

"Because, Francesca," he'd say, "no one who wants to hurt you will stop if you cry. They'll only stop if you make them."

She'd lean back on the wooden bench in the sauna and listen to his voice through the closed door.

"You're small, but you're tough." He'd laugh. "I've got the scars to prove it."

And Francesca would smile, just a little, picturing the miniscule red mark on his left temple where she'd managed to kick him, totally by accident. They were walking down the street and she had tripped over a curb. When he reached down to stop her from falling, she'd kicked him in the head.

C.J. wasn't small. He was a monster. Six foot six and as broad as he was tall. He didn't only have to duck when he walked through a doorway, he had to turn sideways as well. And he worried about Francesca.

The lessons were his way of making sure that she was as safe as possible in the life she chose to lead. He didn't agree with that life but he'd given up arguing about it with her long before. He salved his conscience by refusing to charge her for lessons.

"Francesca," he said, "I'm happy to work with you but I'm not charging you for the lessons."

"C.J...."

"No." He held up his huge hand. "No. Do not even try to give me money."

He stood for a few moments, his bulk blocking out the light from the window, while he waited for her to consider his ultimatum. And then a smile lit up his face.

"Francesca? No money, okay?"

She sighed and said, "No money," but she promised herself that some day she would pay him back for everything he had given her, for all the years he'd protected her. Some day...

So, because C.J. was her friend and he wanted to help her, but mostly because she was often scared, she took the free lessons and she worked her butt off to prove to C.J. that she appreciated the time he spent with her.

It wasn't easy for Francesca to accept anything. She'd spent most of her life being poor while everyone around her—including C.J. and Susannah—were rich. Or at least rich in Francesca's eyes.

They had new clothes for school in September, new clothes for Christmas, for Easter, for each new season. They never wore hand-me-downs or rode secondhand bikes. They went to camp in the summer. They had new three-ring binders for each class and handfuls of colored pencils and pens.

Francesca learned to take nothing from them.

She accepted that she'd have to sit in the cafeteria and eat her peanut-butter-and-jam sandwich while C.J. and Susannah stood in line and bought pizza or hamburgers and chocolate milk. Francesca drank water.

And eventually, they learned not to offer her anything.

"I love peanut butter and jam," she'd say, eating it for the fifth time in a week.

She'd scrape off the green spots in the bread and hide them under her napkin while C.J. and Susannah turned away. One year—Francesca was pretty sure it was grade seven—the two of them brought peanut-butter-and-jam sandwiches for lunch every single day. They drank water with her and walked her home when she didn't have money to take the bus.

C.J. and Francesca and Susannah met in fifth grade and no matter what had happened, they stuck together. They stuck together through C.J.'s stint in the army, through Susannah's society marriage and brilliantly photographed and extremely ugly divorce.

They stuck together even after Francesca left home and started moving. She moved thirty-six times in the twenty years before she moved to this town. She moved from neighborhood to neighborhood, from city to city, from state to state.

Susannah and C.J. stuck with her through all those times. They drove to see her. They flew to see her. They used their holidays to visit her in some small forgotten town and never once complained about it.

And for the few months she lived in the same town as C.J., he trained her.

The two of them visited Francesca in every one of the grungy rooms she lived in over the years; grown-up now, they offered her money, help and jobs but were never offended when she refused. Susannah had always, always, always, been there for those Sunday night phone calls.

Susannah and C.J. were her family and she missed them desperately.

But she couldn't call either of them now. They were on their honeymoon. And she couldn't be happier for them. Or lonelier for herself.

She turned her head at the sound of footsteps on the floor behind her but couldn't crane her neck enough to see anything more than black shoes.

"Young lady," a deep voice spoke. "What are you doing on my floor?"

Francesca blinked and struggled to sit up.

"Wait, let me give you a hand."

He was tall, almost as tall as C.J., but thin to the point of gaunt. And he was old, very old. The shadow she saw against the light made Francesca think of Uriah Heep and she shrank back against the display case.

He bent his knees, crouched down on the floor in front of her. He wasn't anything at all like Uriah Heep, not slimy or ugly or mean. He held out his hands as if he was waiting for her to make the first move. She looked into his eyes, expecting...

Whatever it was she'd been expecting to see, his eyes weren't it. They were the color of willow leaves at the first sign of spring. Francesca almost believed she could see right through them into another world, a world where she hadn't just spent an hour running for her life, a world where she didn't live in a ratty one-room apartment and where she didn't have to work two jobs just to get by.

She looked at those eyes again and reached out her hands to his. He smiled and the smile contained all the delights of a perfect summer's morning.

He pulled her from the floor and guided her over to a chair. Somehow he knew to put her at the table farthest away from the door and to sit her with her back against a wall. And then he did something extraordinary.

The tall man walked slowly over to the door, locked it and turned the sign to Closed. He pulled the shades down over the windows and turned the neon off.

"Hot chocolate, I think," he said as he turned back toward Francesca.

He raised his voice a little.

"Marta? Two hot chocolates, please." He looked over at Francesca with a lopsided grin on his face. "One with extra marshmallows."

CHAPTER 7

The chairs in Bains Candies were comfortable. Francesca hadn't expected that, nor had she expected to be sitting here with a large mug of hot chocolate warming her hands. The woman who'd brought the hot chocolate hadn't said anything, but she'd smiled at Francesca before she'd returned to wherever she'd come from.

The man had looked up, said, "Thanks, Marta," and reached out to touch her hand. She'd returned to him a smile so sweet Francesca had had to turn away. That smile was not meant to be public.

The tall thin man had settled himself in the chair opposite Francesca and was concentrating on his mug. She did the same. Her mug was white with cobalt-blue stripes. His was blue with white stripes. The hot chocolate smelled rich and creamy underneath the layers of marshmallows.

"Joshua," a harsh voice whispered behind Francesca. "The girl needs a towel. She's shivering."

The woman sat down next to Francesca and handed her a towel. It, too, was white with blue stripes and it was warm, as if it had just come from the dryer. It smelled faintly of lavender.

"Your hair is dripping into your hot chocolate. Wrap the towel around your head."

Francesca had to look right at the woman to hear her words. When she had the towel wrapped around her head, she turned to the woman.

"I'm Francesca Bond. Thank you for the towel. I'll just finish my drink—" she gestured at the hot chocolate "—and be on my way."

"No."

The woman turned to the tall man as if to say *you talk to her.* With her head turned, Francesca saw why talking was so difficult. The woman had scars all around her neck, thick ropy scars as if her head had almost been sheared from her body. They were old scars but they were still red and angry.

Francesca wondered how the woman had lived through whatever accident had caused those scars. She wondered why the woman didn't hide the ruin of her throat. And she mostly wondered why she looked so happy.

Francesca waited for the man to speak. She didn't have much choice but to wait, she couldn't move. Not yet. The shivering—which she couldn't stop—sapped whatever energy she'd had.

She took another sip of the hot chocolate, using two hands to lift the cup to her lips. It was sweet and Francesca could feel the sugar beginning to surge through her body, temporarily lifting her spirits, although she knew that she would soon be unable to speak. She needed to finish her drink and find a way to get home.

"Francesca? My name's Joshua Bains. This is my store—" he turned to the woman "—and Marta's."

He smiled at both women and Francesca could see how Marta, obviously much younger than Joshua and beautiful despite her ravaged throat, had fallen for him. His smile was amazing. Warm and sweet and kind and… Well, everything, really.

Marta looked at him again and cleared her throat.

"Ah, yes. Marta's going to help you upstairs and you're going to take a hot shower and get changed. Marta will find you something to wear."

Francesca shook her head.

"I just need a few minutes to get warmed up," she said. "I'll be fine."

"Maybe you will be fine, and maybe not. But I will not send anyone out into a night like this."

As if to emphasize his point, a thunderous roar

clapped overhead, followed quickly by a flash of lightning. Francesca heard the wind pick up, rattling the windows and the shutters. The lights in the store flickered and then died.

"Hold on," Joshua said into the darkness. "There are candles behind the counter."

Francesca heard a scrape against the floor as he pushed the chair back, then a quiet "ouch" as Joshua ran into something in the dark.

The sulfur smell of a wooden match being struck, and then a faint flickering light appeared at the other side of the room. She watched as Joshua lit first one, then two, then three candles. The room lightened, imperceptibly at first, and then it was bright enough for Francesca to see Joshua behind the counter and Marta, now standing next to her with her arm around Francesca's shoulder.

Joshua walked carefully back across the room, the three candles held in his hands. He gave one to Marta and another to Francesca.

"I need to go out back and check the generator," he said. "It won't handle the lights, but we need to keep the refrigeration on."

Francesca trembled at the thought of going back into the storm, but she forced herself from her chair.

"Thanks for the hot chocolate," she said. "I should get going now."

Marta pressed her hand down harder on Francesca's shoulder, pushing her back into the chair. *Sit*, she gestured.

"Wait," she whispered, her voice only just audible over the roar of the storm. "Wait until Joshua comes back."

Marta didn't know what to do. She couldn't talk to Francesca, that wasn't her job. Her job was to provide support for Joshua. She'd seldom had to deal with anyone on her own since the accident and she cursed her lack of communication skills. She needed to make Francesca stay until Joshua came back from checking the generator.

"Francesca?" she whispered, leaning closer. She forced her voice through her vocal cords and out into the world. "I came here on a night just like this," she said.

Marta took a deep breath and ordered her thoughts. She was going to have to tell this story in the fewest possible words or she'd lose her voice. And once she'd overused it, it might be days before she could say another word.

So she went right to the heart of the story.

"I was desperate. So desperate I came to this part of town to buy a gun. I was going to kill myself.

"I bought the gun and scurried into this alley to find a corner where no one would notice me."

She couldn't stop the coughing. *Damn*, she thought, *I don't know if I can make it*.

Francesca scrambled to her feet.

"Water? Marta? Quick, where's the tap? I'll get you a glass of water."

Francesca's face was blurry but Marta tried to focus. Water. That's what she needed. Water.

Marta waved at the biggest glass case and tried to stop the hacking cough. If she couldn't stop, she'd be out of commission for too long. She felt her head start to spin and knew that she was close to fainting.

But a chilly hand pressed a glass of water into hers, helped her lift it to her mouth, and held the glass while Marta drank. She sipped carefully at first. Just once she had gulped the water and almost choked to death as it spewed back out from her constricted throat.

Once her eyes stopped tearing up, Marta took the glass from Francesca and smiled her thanks. She didn't think she'd be able to finish her story. When she'd told it to Joshua, it had taken her months to get the whole story told. And it wasn't that long.

Each night, they'd closed the shop and sat down at this same table. Joshua poured her a glass of wine and himself a scotch and then he waited while she corralled her thoughts into some kind of order. She didn't want to waste a word.

Some nights she got out a single sentence, others she might manage a whole paragraph. But Joshua sat patiently through all those months while she struggled to tell him why she was still going to kill herself despite his care.

She wanted him to know that it wasn't his fault. She wanted him to understand that her life was so desperate there was nothing he could do to help her. All he could do was postpone the inevitable end.

He had taken the gun from her hand and put it away.

As the months progressed, and her story got told, she had realized that she no longer needed the gun. Her life would be lived at Mystic Hearts. She owed Joshua; she owed the house.

So now, for Joshua, for Mystic Hearts, for Francesca, Marta took a deep breath and tried to continue her story.

"Joshua found me with the gun at my temple. He didn't touch me, just talked to me. I never knew a man could talk that much.

"He talked for hours, until the rain stopped and the darkness started to lift. He held out his hand and I gave him the gun. He brought me into the store and made me eat."

She smiled across the room at Joshua puttering behind the cases of candy.

"He saved my life that night. And then he taught me how to live a new one."

Joshua raised his head. Even in the darkness he seemed to understand that Marta wanted him.

He paused by the table and rubbed his hand against Marta's shoulder.

"You ladies need some more hot chocolate," Joshua said. "I'll be right back."

Marta watched Francesca while he was gone. She wasn't shivering anymore but her fingers were tapping on the table, and her legs jiggled under the white cloth. Marta would take no chances.

She pulled her chair closer and placed one hand on Francesca's knee. She rubbed her hand in tiny circles on the girl's knee, with just enough pressure to bring comfort, not pain.

The legs stopped jiggling but her fingers still tapped. Marta moved closer until their thighs were touching and she felt the warmth of her body spreading to Francesca. The warmth wasn't enough. The fingers still tapped. The girl was ready to run.

Marta placed her other hand over the chilled hands on the table. She began to hum. Marta had learned since the accident that when she hummed nothing could go wrong. It was as relaxing as a hot bath or a late summer afternoon.

Marta felt the tension leave the girl's body. She relaxed against the back of her chair, her hands loose on the white cloth.

Joshua had a curious look on his face when he returned to the table, a laden tray in his hands. Marta shook her head at him, signaling, *Don't ask.*

He winked back at her and said, "I've brought sandwiches, soup, hot chocolate, and lemon meringue pie. I know it's not really lemon meringue pie weather. Lemon meringue pie is for warm, sunny evenings, not cold, rainy ones. But I don't care. It was in the pie case and it was exactly what I wanted."

He set the tray on the next table over and started unloading it, filling the small round table with food and drinks. Two plates of dainty sandwiches went in the middle, three bowls of steaming, fragrant soup were carefully placed in front of Marta, Francesca and Joshua. A large silver pot and three clean mugs filled the empty spaces. He left the pie on the other table.

"Eat," he said, "eat. It's late and cold and wet and we're safe inside. Let's enjoy it."

Marta smiled at Joshua and whispered, "When we're finished eating, you need to tell Francesca the story."

CHAPTER 8

"Marta grew up in Amsterdam," he said, and then paused. He wanted to tell the story as he'd heard it.

"She grew up in Amsterdam," Joshua said, replicating as closely as he could Marta's words. "And for a time, she was an opera singer.

"Her career and her life were interchangeable. Both of them ran like a Japanese bullet train, fast and always ahead of schedule. She won every competition she entered, got every part she auditioned for, made more money than she'd ever expected, seduced every man she might have wanted."

Marta's sleepy smile grew into a grin. Joshua bowed and continued.

"She abandoned her family. They gave her everything and she took it, offering nothing in return, not even money, of which she had plenty, and especially not love.

"She made *the* decision the day of her thirty-eighth birthday. It was ten o'clock on a beautiful morning, a warm spring day in Tuscany. She was alone.

"She dressed in her sexiest chiffon and highest heels, grabbed the keys to the van that usually carried her luggage and hurried out of the villa. If she drove quickly, she could be in Cannes that evening.

"Bet you could see it coming, couldn't you? '*Pride goeth before a fall,*' and in her case, no truer words would be spoken."

Joshua stopped. Marta listened to his breath, harsh in his chest. She knew that he didn't want to tell the next part of the story.

"Joshua," Marta said, her voice rough and barely audible across the tiny table. "Finish the story. Please. Francesca needs to hear it and I can't do it myself."

It was the darkest part of the night, that time when every sound seemed magnified a thousand times. The rain hit the windows with a clear *ping* for each drop. The refrigerators hummed along with the generator and the old house creaked in the wind.

"Joshua?" Marta repeated his name.

"I'll finish the story tomorrow," he said, voice shaking with the strain of what was to come.

"No. Tonight. You have to do it tonight."

Marta knew they would have only one chance with Francesca. She thought, although she didn't tell Joshua, Francesca might be leaving them in the morning. If she didn't hear the story now, she would go.

"Tell her."

"I don't need to know this." Francesca pushed her chair back from the table and started to stand up.

Marta pointed at Joshua.

"Tell her. Now."

She turned to grab Francesca's hand, now warm and soft.

"Sit," she said between panting breaths. "Down. I want you to hear this story."

Francesca sat in her chair and waited while Joshua and Marta had some silent exchange. She knew the exchange was about her and she wondered why it was so important to Marta that she hear the story.

"It's none of my business," Francesca said to Marta. "I really don't need to hear it."

What she meant was that she didn't *want* to hear it, didn't want to be responsible for someone else's pain and sorrow, didn't want to know someone else's life, not like that. Her own was complicated enough.

Joshua tore his gaze away from Marta, turned

to Francesca and answered the question she hadn't dared ask.

"Marta wants you to listen because only one person knows who she is, who she has been, why she's here. Marta has no children, no nieces and nephews. I am too old, much older than she. But Marta is the last of the Van Iperens and she has no one else to whom she can leave the story."

Marta nodded encouragingly, patting Francesca on the shoulder.

Francesca couldn't help herself, blurting out the words before she could bite her tongue and stop them.

"Is Marta sick?"

She looked away from Marta when she asked the question, not wanting to see the sorrow in Marta's eyes.

Marta sputtered, her equivalent of a belly laugh.

"I'm not sick." She waved a hand at Joshua, ordering him to continue for her.

"Marta's never been sick a day in her life. Not sick like that, anyway."

"Sick like what?" Francesca asked.

"Sick like dying," Joshua replied.

Francesca gestured at her own throat. "But…" she said, "what about…?"

"How she got those scars is a big part of the story. That's part of what Marta wants you to know."

Joshua smiled at Francesca.

"Are you in?" he asked.

She hesitated and then shrugged her shoulders.

"I guess so," she said, seeing how important the telling of the story was to the two of them. "I've nowhere else to be tonight."

Joshua's voice again lowered and roughened and drew Francesca right back into Marta's story.

"She was about halfway to Cannes, racing alongside the Mediterranean, when a siren caught her attention. A police car appeared in her rearview mirror, lights blinking, siren screaming.

"She ignored the noise and fury and put her foot firmly on the gas. It didn't help. The police car pulled up beside her and the man in the driver's seat motioned her to the side of the road.

"She ignored him, as well, and pushed the gas pedal to the floor.

"The van shook and rattled but it picked up speed until she had left the police car behind. She looked over her shoulder to make sure she was safe and…"

Joshua's voice faltered.

Francesca said, "That's enough. Don't tell me any more."

Marta looked sternly at Joshua, then Francesca, as if to say, *Don't make me tell this story myself*. She didn't touch her throat but she might as well have.

"That's all she remembers. She doesn't remember the accident. She can't remember the next three months.

"She remembers waking to a world of pain. She remembers the doctor telling her that she was lucky to be alive. She didn't feel lucky.

She had lost everything. Her voice. Her career. And even before the accident, her selfishness meant she'd lost her friends. Her family.

But the hospital was justly proud of keeping her alive. She had, so they told her, been hit by a steel girder flying off an overloaded truck.

The girder had practically decapitated her. She lived because the ambulance was following right behind the police car, which was following right behind the van. And she lived because she was three minutes from the hospital and the surgeon on call had spent most of his career in war zones, with plenty of experience with bombing and battlefield injuries.

Marta left the hospital one year and three months after the accident, in perfect physical condition. Except she couldn't talk, not really. And she carried a rope of scars around her throat, bearing witness to her inability to earn a living in the only way she knew.

"She went to America and bought a gun.

"She found a deserted alley. She stood in the rain and raised the gun to her temple.

"Her hands shook, but she was determined. There was nothing to live for.

"And then she heard my voice."

The story echoed in Francesca's ears but she was too tired and too confused to try and decipher it. She closed her eyes and waited.

CHAPTER 9

Marta held out her hand. Francesca, too tired to decide whether she was making a mistake or not, took it. She followed Marta from the shop and up a flight of narrow stairs.

The walls were covered in old-fashioned floral wallpaper, the flowers so faded Francesca couldn't tell what colors or types they had once been. Flowers, old-fashioned and sweet smelling. Violets. Woodbine. Roses. Lilacs. Daisies. Sweetpeas and bachelor's buttons.

She put her hand on the banister. It rippled at her touch, layers of paint reshaping and softening its original form.

The ascent of the narrow, steep stairs felt as if Francesca were climbing Everest or K2, each step a struggle, each foot reaching for the next riser in agony. By the time she hit the top step, she could barely stand.

Marta's back shimmered in the flickering light

cast by the candle she carried. She swayed, as graceful as a dancer as she moved away from Francesca down the hallway.

Francesca wanted to cry out to her. She wanted to slow Marta down but she also wanted to study her movements so that one day when she wasn't so tired, Francesca could learn to move that way.

Because the hours spent in C.J.'s dojo hadn't given her that confident walk, that ability to take over the space around her. It had made her strong, yes, and solid on her feet, but it hadn't given her whatever skill Marta possessed that allowed her to wear the space around her as an accessory, without fear.

Francesca knew all about fear. She'd been scared pretty much all of the time since she'd left home. But what she wanted to know now wasn't about fear, not really.

It was about moving as if you weren't scared. Marta had to be scared sometimes, but she walked as if she owned the space she moved in.

Francesca wanted to spend months studying Marta, watching her move, watching her take possession of her space without using words. She wanted to learn how to feel safe in her own space. If she could do that, maybe she could begin to feel safe in other places, as well.

She collapsed against the faded wallpaper at the top of the stairs and sighed. She wanted to sleep right there.

"Francesca?" Marta's rough voice caressed her like the grooming tongue of a big cat. It tickled.

Marta put the candle down on a chair and came back toward Francesca, shadows flickering in front of her.

Marta slid down to sit next to Francesca on the floor. She smelled of hot chocolate and the faded, sweet scent of long-pressed flowers.

Her voice was barely audible in the darkness and Francesca realized that up until now she had been reading Marta's lips to supplement her hearing. Now, in the darkness, even with Marta right next to her, Francesca strained to make out the words.

"Francesca Bond." A whisper in the darkness. "Can you get up? Your room is right down the hall."

Francesca nodded and then realized that Marta might not have seen her.

"I don't know if I can get up." Francesca hated saying those words but she couldn't move.

"Let me help you."

Francesca heard that loud and clear. *Help* was a trigger word for her. She had spent most of her life making it on her own, refusing assistance from even her closest friends. This time, though, she had no choice unless she wanted to spend the rest of the night on her butt on the floor.

She cleared her throat. Did it again. And again. Finally, unable to think of another way out of the mess, she said, quietly, "Help me up, please."

Marta rose and slipped her hands under Francesca's elbows. She lifted her to her feet, seemingly without effort.

The hallway swirled around Francesca. She felt light-headed and heavy-hearted at the same time. She hated being sick, hated needing help, hated being helpless. But the whole night had been like that, so why should now be any different?

She swayed against Marta, whose strong right arm came around her waist.

"Come on," she said. "We need to get you to your room."

"My room," she whispered. "It's not my room."

Marta shrugged. "Names are what we make of them," she said.

Francesca's quick anger rose at that cryptic statement but she was too tired to fight about it. In her opinion, names made things. If you labeled someone stupid or lazy or vicious, that's how they turned out.

She'd been labeled.

She was a dropout.

No matter how many classes she took after she'd quit high school, how many certificates she pinned to her wall, how many books she read or papers she wrote, she was still a dropout with all that implied.

She was stupid.

She was lazy.

She was uneducated.

She was poor.

It hadn't taken Francesca very long to understand that being poor didn't mean just that. When someone got labeled poor, poverty included, without exception, laziness and stupidity.

But most of the people in her neighborhood worked hard to pay the rent and buy enough groceries to get by. And maybe some of her neighbors were uneducated, but very few of them were stupid.

Francesca leaned a little more heavily against Marta. Her legs would collapse under her if she didn't sit down soon. The time sitting at the table in the shop had tricked her into believing she was okay.

She wasn't.

And now that she was back on her feet, it was more than obvious.

The soles of her feet stung with each step she took. The blisters she'd gotten while running had burst and then scabbed over, and now, as she staggered down the hallway, they were bursting again. This time, Francesca knew, it wasn't clear liquid soaking into her socks—it was blood.

Francesca put her right foot on the floor and grimaced. Her feet felt as if she had been walking in burning sand. For hours.

And her calf muscles screamed at her. *Stop moving. Stop right now. We're going to pop if you don't stop.*

Francesca tried to ignore the lower half of her body, but her ankles lurched over when she moved, her thighs quivered, and the top half of her body wasn't in any better shape. Her eyelids twitched, her head ached, her throat felt rough and raw. Her shoulders and neck felt as if she'd spent the day carrying twenty-five pound bags of potatoes from truck to pantry.

But she kept moving. The words *your room* drew her onward. Marta's sweet scent gave her hope.

"Soon," she whispered, her head dropping to Marta's shoulder. "Soon I'll be able to lie down."

Marta opened the door to the room at the end of hallway.

"There are clean towels in the bathroom," she said, pointing to a small door set into the wall. "And there's lots of hot water."

She pulled a bottle of aspirin from her pocket.

"Take a couple of these before you go to bed. You'll feel better in the morning."

When the door closed behind Marta, Francesca collapsed onto the bed.

"Oh my God," she said. "Oh my God."

She rubbed her hand over the soft white chenille spread, and leaned back against the pillows piled against the headboard. She grinned weakly at the lilacs and yellow roses on the wallpaper.

"I'm imagining you, but I don't care."

She touched the chenille again, as if that touch would make the whole room real.

A fever, that's what it was. This wasn't, couldn't be, the exact room she'd imagined all those hours ago in the rain.

She didn't really see the sheepskin rug, or the rocking chair. The faded wooden floors were all in her mind, as was the bookshelf next to the bed.

Francesca toed off her shoes, carefully pulled her damp and bloody socks from her blistered feet, put the totally gross twenty-dollar bill on the bedside table (it was getting washed with her laundry this week) and swung her legs off the bed and into the softest, warmest, coziest rug ever made.

That's how she knew it wasn't real. No rug could be as soft as the one she'd pictured in her mind. She didn't care if it wasn't real, she enjoyed the feel of it on her sore feet anyway.

The tiny door set into the wall drew her. The

glass knob creaked as it turned. She pulled the door toward her.

A bathroom. Pale yellow, she thought, though she couldn't be sure in the candlelight. A claw-footed bathtub and deep green towels.

Francesca shook her head and then leaned into the mirror above the sink.

"You're delirious," she said to the woman in the mirror. "You need to take some aspirin, go back out there and get under the covers. You'll be fine in the morning."

Francesca was pretty sure that the whole Bains Candies thing was a dream. In fact, now that she thought more carefully about it, she was pretty sure she was in a hospital somewhere.

Concussed. That was it. She'd been running away from those men and she'd fallen and hit her head. Someone must have found her and called an ambulance.

She ignored the towels, the candlelight, the scent of lavender, and concentrated.

"Check your pockets, Francesca," she mumbled to herself. "See if your keys are still there."

She patted the pockets in her jeans. Keys. Check. Small wallet. Check. No money. Check. She hadn't any to start with except the twenty-dollar bill in her shoe.

She sat down on the floor and reached for the towel. She lifted it to her nose. Lavender. Definitely not disinfectant. Francesca hadn't been in many hospitals but she couldn't believe that any of them had deep green towels smelling of lavender.

Okay, she really was in a room that exactly duplicated the room she'd imagined hours ago.

She touched her hand to her forehead.

"You must have a fever," she muttered to the mirror. "If your forehead feels okay, it's only because your hands are burning up as well as your forehead."

She twisted the cap off the bottle of aspirin, filled a glass with water and swallowed the bitter pills, flinging her head back as she forced them to the back of her throat.

"There," she said. "That'll fix you."

She pulled off her jeans and T-shirt, both still damp, and hung them over the tub. She unhooked her bra, also damp, and shivered as she removed it.

A chill ran across her shoulders and she started to tremble again.

"I'd better not get sick," she warned the mirror. "I can't afford to take any time off work."

A thick robe of the same dark green as the towels hung beside the sink. Francesca hesitated, then wrapped it around herself.

For this one night, she would pretend that this room was hers.

So she explored the medicine cabinet and the cupboard beneath the sink. She rummaged through the linens neatly piled on the shelves behind the door. She used the soap and the toothbrush next to the sink.

She washed her feet, then took the first-aid kit from beneath the sink. She slathered them with Polysporin and wrapped them in facecloths from the linen shelves.

By this time, Francesca had given up worrying about whether she should use the contents of the room.

She opened the shampoo and took a deep breath. It smelled of green apples.

And then she explored the bedroom.

She scrunched her toes into the sheepskin rug, sat down in the rocking chair, ran her fingers through the bowl of potpourri. She opened the white curtains at the window and looked out at the rain.

She opened the door to the hallway, then the door set in the opposite wall. An empty closet, wooden hangers waiting to be filled, and smelling of cedar and lavender.

She opened each drawer of the dresser beneath

the window. More lavender, this time in tiny sachets tied with purple ribbons.

There were a few pairs of panties in the top drawer, still in their wrappers. A cotton sports bra in its box. The underwear was her size. A six-pack of sports socks.

Francesca sat down in the rocking chair and removed the facecloths protecting her feet. She pulled on a pair of cotton socks. They felt warm. She crouched down and looked behind the dresser. A radiator rumbled away, heating up the clothes in the dresser.

The middle drawer contained a few brightly colored T-shirts and a pair of faded jeans. She checked the labels. They were all her size.

The bottom drawer held sweaters. Home-knit sweaters in blues and greens and golds. Francesca pulled one from the drawer and held it up against her. It, too, would fit.

She picked up the candle and followed the walls around the room. There were pictures everywhere.

A castle set in deep purple heather.

A black dog and a ginger kitten.

A hill filled with daffodils and poppies and two little girls carrying white parasols.

And every one of them framed in gold.

Francesca had saved the best for last. The bed

beckoned but she was unable to resist the bookshelf filled with books.

She sat down again in the rocking chair and looked at the books for a few minutes. Then she touched the spines. They looked old, the print faded and worn from years of handling.

She lifted one from the shelf, held it to her nose and sneezed. Once. Twice. And then again.

Francesca dropped the book onto her lap and sniffled until the sneezes retreated.

The paper felt soft and dusty beneath her fingertips, the title deeply embossed into the cracked leather. The color was gone from the embossing, but Francesca carefully ran her fingers across the letters.

The Keeper of the Bees by Gene Stratton-Porter.

She clutched the book to her chest, remembering her grandmother. She'd read that book over and over again, sitting in the cool basement in the hot summer afternoons. She wanted to be Scout. She wanted to smell the sand and the horses. She wanted to laugh with the children of many colors. She wanted, more than anything, to live in a world with a happy ending. Because she was pretty sure her life wasn't going to have one.

The book had been her grandmother's and it, along with almost a dozen others, had sat on a rickety old shelf in the spare room in the basement.

There'd been an uncomfortable sofa with springs that had stuck into Francesca's butt, a table that had lost one of its legs so it had been propped up on a couple of cinder blocks, an old lamp that had lost its shade.

Francesca had begged a blanket from her grandmother. She'd ended up with a much-mended and baby-soft blanket that her grandmother had inherited from her mother. Francesca still had the blanket. She kept it in her closet, packed in a plastic bag with cedar chips for company. She removed it once a month, refolded it so the creases would be in different places and the blanket wouldn't start to decay.

Francesca hadn't had a security blanket as a baby; she hadn't needed one. But now her grandmother's blanket, along with her grandfather's candy tins, provided the only security she knew and she looked after them very very carefully. Because if the blanket were damaged, if she lost the tins, Francesca's ever-so-slight sense of security would disappear.

It had been cool and dark in her grandmother's basement and no one had bothered her there. Her mother, thoroughly pissed off with what she called Francesca's don't-give-a-damn attitude, had ordered her to spend the afternoons helping her grandmother.

Grandma didn't need any help. She had her

domain under complete control and she didn't want any interference with it, so she pointed Francesca to the basement and the few books in it and told her to come back upstairs when it was time to set the table for dinner.

That summer, Francesca read those dozen books—all old-fashioned stories her grandmother had acquired as a teenager—many times. She'd start with the book at the left-hand side of the bookshelf, and read each book in order, beginning with *The Keeper of the Bees* and ending with Lamb's *Tales from Shakespeare*.

She never got bored, never wished for more books. Each book had been a different world for Francesca and she'd lived every single one of them over and over again.

She had spent much of her adult life trying to replace those books. She didn't remember the names and authors of all of them but she knew she'd recognize them when she found them. She haunted secondhand bookstores and thrift shops. She hung out in old age homes, hoping that the women residing there would have the same taste in books as her grandmother did.

She had eleven books lined up on the shelf beside her bed at home, eleven out of twelve. And now here was the final book.

She climbed into bed, wrapped the chenille spread around her shoulders, sank deep into the feather pillow, placed the book beside her on a pillow of its own, and wondered if Marta would let her take it home with her.

Francesca shut her eyes but couldn't sleep. She kept opening them to check and make sure the room was still there, and still the same. She touched the book several times for the same reason.

She blew out the candle around dawn and fell asleep as the sun began to light the windows.

CHAPTER 10

Midsummer Day

The heat of the sun against her right cheek brought Francesca to dull consciousness. Her other cheek was dented from sleeping with her face on the book.

She lifted her head from the pillow and groaned. She'd fallen asleep, she thought, somewhere near dawn but those few hours of unconsciousness had done little to heal her muscles.

She curled her feet, first down, then up.

"Ouch."

"Francesca?" A raspy voice whispered from the door. "Are you awake?"

"Not sure. I'll test it."

She stretched her legs out and her calves screamed in protest. She wasn't sure which hurt worse, her feet or her calves, but she was betting on the feet. The calves were likely to loosen up if she used them; the feet—she curled them again and cringed as the blisters started to seep—were likely to get worse if she stood up.

But she couldn't stay in bed all day, especially in a bed that wasn't her own. She was already late for work. Swinging her feet over the side, Francesca scrunched her shoulders, locked her teeth together so she wouldn't cry out, and put her feet down on the sheepskin.

The sheepskin didn't help.

Even the slightest touch of the soles of her feet to the soft wool radiated excruciating pain up from her toes right into her jawbone. She couldn't restrain a whimper.

Marta slammed open the door, hurried across the room and knelt at Francesca's side.

"God, girl, you're a mess. Wait right here. I'm going to get some warm water and Epsom salts. Aspirin, too. Don't move."

"I've got to get going. I need to be at work—" she glanced at the clock "—now."

Marta threw a look over her shoulder that promised nothing. Francesca lay back on the bed and moaned.

"Marta," she projected her voice across the room, "I really do have to go to work. We need to figure out a way that I can put my shoes back on. I can't afford to miss a shift."

Marta didn't answer or, if she did, Francesca didn't hear her. She simply appeared carrying a steaming pan, a glass of water and the first-aid kit.

The first aid was quick and painful. The Epsom salts stung like hell and Marta didn't waste much time being careful with Francesca's feet. She just dipped them into the hot water, said, "Keep them there until I say you're done," and watched while Francesca screamed.

Ten minutes later her feet were lobster-red and the pain was bearable. Marta wrapped them in moleskin, pulled a new pair of cotton socks over the bandaging, and helped Francesca up.

"We'll bathe them again later on," she said. "The trick is to keep them clean and well wrapped."

"I won't be here later on, Marta. I can't be."

Marta ignored her.

"Get dressed and come downstairs for breakfast. Joshua's making pancakes."

"I hate pancakes," Francesca muttered.

Marta's voice might be damaged, but her hearing was as sharp as a five-year-old and her tone as tough as any mother's.

"These are Joshua's famous blueberry pancakes and he only makes them one day a year. Get dressed and get downstairs."

Marta's glare convinced her. Francesca stepped

gingerly onto the sheepskin rug. Bearable. Just. She scrambled under the bedspread for the book, then found her clothes, clean and pressed, laid out on the rocking chair.

Francesca would stay for breakfast and then catch the nearest bus.... She turned to the window. She wasn't quite sure where she was, though she knew she wasn't that far from the coffee shop. She hadn't run for that long, had she? No. She had to be, at most, an hour's walking distance from home, so maybe fifteen minutes by bus, no farther than that. She couldn't be.

But when she pulled back the lace curtains, Francesca saw a world as completely different from the one she knew as it was possible to be.

The cobblestone street gleamed russet in the sunlight. Cherry trees bloomed, forming the palest of pink canopies over the stones. The slightest gust of wind caused a cascade of blossoms to drift down to the street, pink snowflakes piling up against the curbs. Beautiful summer and no sign at all of the roaring storm of last night.

The streetlights appeared to have been sculpted in the 1890s, wrought-iron curlicues and gaslight bulbs taking turns with the cherry trees to hang over the sidewalks.

And the houses?

They were all Victorian, covered with gingerbread and spindles and even some turrets. They sported bay windows and stained glass and extravagant paint. The one directly across the street combined turquoise, yellow and a pale peach color.

Francesca scanned the whole street, not a neon sign in sight. She looked down at the front of the house she was in.

A green-and-white striped awning, a cat sprawled contentedly on the sidewalk in the sun. No neon visible. She looked up at the peak of the roof. No neon there, either.

Francesca closed her eyes and pressed her forehead against the window. She tried to swallow her fear but knew it would be impossible. She risked another look. Beautiful, yes, but not the dank alley she had scurried into last night.

"I sure ain't in Kansas anymore," she said to the window.

Francesca tried to laugh but what came out of her mouth was a faint, strangled scream.

She had read too many novels, too much science fiction and fantasy and horror not to understand the possibilities. She could be anywhere.

A parallel universe, good or bad.

Down a rabbit hole.

Transported to another time.

In a movie, probably one made in the 1950s.

In a photograph or a painting.

In another dimension.

In a book.

Francesca chose the book. She would be in one of those saccharine-sweet romances written in the nineteenth century. It made sense. Those books were full of:

Lace curtains.

Victorian houses.

Cobblestones.

No trash.

Children playing in the street without supervision.

People walking rather than driving.

No bus stops in sight.

And the astonishing gardens. They spilled over onto the sidewalks, filled with random color and greenery. Francesca couldn't recognize even half of the plants she saw from her window, despite having spent a few weeks struggling through a book on gardening.

It was the perfect Victorian street in a city that was anything but. Francesca's city wasn't clean or innocent or safe. Francesca's city was dark and dirty and frightening.

She stepped away from the window. Closed her eyes and took five deep breaths. That wasn't quite enough. She took another five. Now.

She returned to the window, keeping her eyes on the floor, sneaking up on the view.

"Damn. Damn. Damn."

The street hadn't changed. Wherever Francesca found herself, it was more than just a momentary delusion. Her delusion had legs.

So she was just going to have to run with it. At least until she finished the blueberry pancakes she smelled from the shop.

She put *The Keeper of the Bees* back onto the bookshelf, not without some serious twinges of regret. But the book belonged here. Francesca knew how much the book should cost; she'd been checking it out in the small dark hours of the night when she was at work at the Mouse. She regularly searched several antique-book and auction sites.

She couldn't afford that book, not right now.

She contemplated another job, but the thought of it made her feel sicker than she already did. She was at her limit now, maybe even slightly past it.

She remembered last night and then tried to shrug it off, both the escape and Bains Candies. It was time to get back to the real world.

Francesca adamantly ignored the fact that she had absolutely no idea of how she was going to do that. She was stuck in some parallel universe and she didn't have the ruby slippers to get home with.

Blueberry pancakes, first. Then figure out how to get home. Joshua and Marta would know. But would they tell her?

The banister felt solid beneath her hand, not as solid as Marta, but stable enough for Francesca to get to the main floor on her own.

She'd put on her sneakers, pulled her hair back in a ponytail, and replaced the grimy, stained twenty-dollar bill in her right instep.

"Coffee?" Joshua's cheerful voice filled the shop.

"Please. Just black."

It hurt Francesca to accept coffee and breakfast and most especially a room from these people but at the time each separate thing was offered, she'd felt she had no choice.

There was no way she could have gone back out into the rain last night; no way she would be able to get home without eating something this morning.

But Francesca made a note to herself to remember she had been enchanted. The house, Marta and Joshua, the shop, and the room. *The Keeper of the Bees*. Sheepskin rug.

Add all of those things together and she couldn't resist. She tucked the note to herself into the front of her brain and colored it lime-green. She added a few exclamation marks and several DO NOT

FORGET signs and posted a large crossing guard carrying a sign with a big red X. X marked the spot.

Enchanted. Francesca had been enchanted. And she was not happy about it at all, even if it had happened on Midsummer eve. She lived in the *real* world, hard, unforgiving and mostly frightening. Magic couldn't make it any easier, any safer. People used drugs or sex or alcohol to make the *real* world disappear. Magic was just another form of forgetting. Magic—of any kind—made Francesca angry.

Marta and Joshua didn't seem to notice the disgruntled expression that had settled on Francesca's face. They were as cheerful as the birds outside the window.

Marta smiled at Francesca and helped her to a chair. The CLOSED sign still graced the front door despite the half a dozen children hopping impatiently on the sidewalk in front of the shop windows.

A napkin, a coffee and a plate piled high with hot pancakes. Joshua sat down opposite her and Marta leaned against the wall beside him.

"How are you this morning, Francesca?" Joshua asked, pushing a jar of maple syrup across the table.

"I'm fine. I need to thank—"

Joshua held up his hand.

"No need to thank us. We loved having you. We—"

Marta slapped a hand on his shoulder and he stopped in the middle of the sentence.

Francesca mentally shrugged. No odder than anything else. The candy store, all storybook perfection, remained the same as the night before. Francesca had hoped that somehow, while she'd slept, it would have transformed itself into something that made sense, something recognizable. Something that belonged in her world.

It hadn't.

Francesca couldn't bear to ask the questions racing through her head. She didn't want to hear the answers. She ignored the voice in the back of her head chanting, *It's the House. You're in the House*.

Joshua grinned at her as if he could read her thoughts.

"Don't thank us," he repeated. "We're happy you're here."

Marta nodded her agreement and pulled over another chair. She took a cushion from the wooden chest beside her and placed it on the seat.

"Put your feet up, you'll feel better."

Francesca rested her feet on the chair and concentrated on the pancakes. She wasn't sure when she'd eaten before the few bites she'd managed last night but it had been a while.

She counted backward on her fingers.

Breakfast yesterday? Nope, she'd been late for work. Lunch? Nope, two people had called in sick, no time for a break. Dinner? Nope. Same excuse.

Go back another day. Nine o'clock watercolor class, no time for breakfast. Work at one, just time to make it from campus to work, no time for lunch. Off at eight, half an hour to make it to job number two, no time for dinner and no food on site.

Internet cafés carried every kind of caffeine known to man but food was very much a secondary consideration. No food, and no money for takeout.

Francesca was pretty sure that she'd eaten something in the last couple of days. She couldn't remember what it was, but she was sure she'd had dinner. She was quite sure she remembered cooking something. Pasta, probably, and tomato sauce and maybe even some leftover chicken strips from the coffee shop.

But she'd had hot chocolate and a taste of soup, sandwiches and lemon meringue pie last night.

She dripped a smidgen of maple syrup onto the pile of stained blue pancakes on her plate and then figured, what the hell? She lifted the jar, pulled back the spout and poured. And poured. And poured.

Her pancakes were soaked with syrup. She looked up. Joshua's eyes were gleaming. Marta looked surprised, then smiled as Francesca lifted the first forkful to her mouth.

"I told you," she said, pride clear in her ravaged voice. "Joshua's blueberry pancakes are..." She paused. "There isn't a word for them."

Francesca held the first bite in her mouth and savored the flavors. Blueberries, plump and sweet. They popped under the pressure of her teeth. Maple syrup, rich and thick and heavenly. The salty bite of butter and the dense warmth of the batter. She'd never eaten anything so good.

"Francesca?" Joshua leaned over the table until his face was only a few inches from hers. "What are you going to do today?"

She swallowed the pancake she was chewing, forked up another bite and swallowed that one as well. She couldn't help herself.

"Francesca?" he asked again.

"I'm going to finish my breakfast, give you the twenty dollars that's in my sock, and then I'm going to take a bus to work. You do have buses, don't you?"

She took another bite, then another. The maple syrup beckoned and she poured another dollop onto the remaining pancakes.

"I have to be at work—" she looked at her watch "—right now. I'm late."

"You don't have to go. The room is empty and you could stay here and help us with the store."

Joshua knew he'd made a mistake the minute he saw the expression on Francesca's face. It had changed from complete and utter bliss to fear in less than the time it took for him to say the words.

Marta patted his shoulder. She'd seen the fear, too.

He backtracked.

"Francesca, there's something you need to know."

Marta squeezed his shoulder, hard. Joshua looked up at her and she shook her head, ever so slightly.

Why not? he signaled, with raised eyebrows.

She's not ready, Marta's eyes said.

How else am I going to keep her here? He grimaced his concern.

"I don't think you can," Marta whispered. "I don't think she's going to stay."

CHAPTER 11

Marta had been right. Francesca out-stubborned them. She insisted on giving Joshua the twenty-dollar bill hidden in her sock and only reluctantly accepted the ten-dollar bill he gave her in exchange; insisted on leaving as soon as she'd finished her breakfast.

"Thank you," she said when she finished her third plate of pancakes and her fourth cup of coffee. "I really have to be going now. How do I get to—" an odd little pause "—to Thirteenth and Main from here? Where's the nearest bus stop?"

"The buses are a few blocks that way," Joshua said, pointing out the door and to the left.

Francesca ignored the giant thump her heart made as she heard those words. A few blocks? She'd barely made it down the stairs.

"It's okay, it's a beautiful day for walking."

And then she tried to ignore the pain in her feet and the oozing into her socks. Mostly, though, she tried to ignore the fear, succeeding well enough to stand up and shuffle toward the door.

She could feel Joshua and Marta watching her, though neither said a word until Marta's faint "Oh, no" when Francesca crumpled, once again, to the black and white tiles.

Joshua turned to Marta and raised his eyebrows and his hands.

"Pick her up, you fool," she whispered. "She needs to go back up to bed."

When he bent down next to Francesca, she moaned.

"Not again," she whispered, her cheek against a black tile. "Not again."

"I don't think you can go home right yet, young lady."

She nodded, unwillingly.

"I'll help you upstairs." Joshua glanced over at Marta. "Just until you feel better," he added, "just a day or so."

Francesca's eyes filled with tears but she shook them away.

"Thanks," she groaned, her voice as reluctant as Marta's on a bad day, "just for a few hours."

Joshua helped Francesca upstairs and left her to Marta's ministrations. He hurried back down the stairs and flipped the sign on the front door to

OPEN. Serving the neighborhood kids who'd made Bains Candies their Saturday-morning stop would take his mind off Francesca, so scared and alone....

Joshua sold chocolates and licorice and caramels, hard candies and soft ones, blue candy and pink. He even sold cotton candy. Always yellow on Saturdays.

The adults waited for the first rush to be over before they arrived for coffee and scones or muffins. They were far less impatient than the little ones. Joshua wondered whether they felt the magic of Mystic Hearts.

Their fists unclenched and their frowns turned into smiles as they crossed the threshold. It didn't seem to matter how stressed they'd been when they'd arrived, by the time Marta showed up at their table with the coffeepot, they were laughing at the funnies rather than growling at the headlines.

Joshua knew that spending sixty years in Mystic Hearts had changed him. He'd arrived in the city in the early spring of 1947, mustered out of Berlin. He'd taken his small savings and had planned to buy himself a sanctuary.

He'd spent the previous five years going from Portland to the East Coast, to Italy, and then to Germany. He didn't have a home anymore. Both his parents had died while he was away, and his brother was killed just after Pearl Harbor.

He left Berlin, landed in New York and hopped onto the first bus out of the city. He wanted to live somewhere in the middle of the country, somewhere safe.

Three months later, tired and discouraged, he got off a bus somewhere in the Midwest. Like all the bus stations he'd seen over the past ninety days, this one squatted in the dirt and disease of the worst part of the city, but Joshua didn't care.

For the first couple of weeks, he'd changed buses at every station, not caring which direction the bus was headed. He went west, then north, then back east, then south. He ate in bus-depot diners, cleaned up in bus-depot bathrooms and listened to the news on bus-depot radios.

He spent most of the first two weeks sleeping. He slept on buses, careful to angle his head toward the window and not the person traveling next to him. He slept on bus-depot benches when his bus pulled in too late to transfer to another until the morning.

The next two weeks he watched. He watched his fellow passengers. Some, like him, were ex-army. But unlike him, they all seemed to have a destination in mind. Unlike him, they were in a hurry to get somewhere.

He watched them race off the bus and into the

arms of their mothers, their sweethearts, their families. And he envied them that love.

He watched women and children hoping to make a new and better life on the other side of the country. It didn't seem to matter whether they were from the west and traveling east, or from the east and traveling west. They believed they were headed for a better place.

He watched young men and he knew they were heading for induction. He wanted to tell them… What? That the army wasn't a good place for young men? That learning to cradle a killing machine in your arms instead of your wife or child wasn't a good way to grow up?

But Joshua told them nothing because for some men the army *was* a good place, a safe and secure place to move into their future.

The war had given him a deep sense of the individuality of the people around him. Everyone wanted something different from their life, everyone yearned for their own particular brand of future.

He traveled this way, watching and waiting, for a few more weeks. He used his voice sparingly during these days. He ordered coffee, bacon and eggs in the morning, soup at lunch, and a beer and a burger for dinner.

Joshua quickly realized that every bus depot in every town and city was a replica of all the others. In fact, he wasn't quite sure if the same five people didn't work in every single bus depot in the whole country.

The short pasty man with thick glasses worked behind every counter. It was obvious he knew the timetable by heart but was unwilling to share his knowledge with the customers. He grudgingly handed them an illegible piece of paper.

"Look it up and come back when you know where you want to go."

There was a maintenance guy who seemed to be long past retirement age, pushing a mop and dragging a filthy bucket of water behind him.

The stained T-shirt worn by the cook in every diner barely met his pants over his big belly. A cigarette hung from his mouth and he was almost, but not quite, bald.

The same two waitresses—one blond and one brunette—worked in the diners. The blond one was generally a little older and a little harder around the edges than the brunette, who was a little less nosy. Both of them chewed gum, spoke in short high-pitched bursts, and promised that their diner had the best apple pie in the country.

"Come on, honey," the blond would say. "You need to eat. You're too thin."

Joshua by this time had figured out that wearing his uniform got him better service but along with that service came curiosity.

"Where you stationed, boy?" That was the bus driver's question.

"You heading home to your sweetheart, Sergeant?" Every waitress asked him, each one with exactly the same note of hope hiding in her voice.

"Do you want some of this fried chicken, son?" asked the old women riding the buses with him. "I made lots, always make too much now," they invariably added. Joshua looked into their sad eyes and accepted a checked napkin, a chicken leg and potato salad.

"What's that medal for?" Every boy he saw asked him that, followed by, "Did you kill anyone?"

Six weeks into the trip, he left the string of bus depots for the first time and walked three blocks over to a Salvation Army thrift store. He bought three pairs of faded jeans, a Yankees baseball cap and a light brown checked jacket.

After that, people mostly let him sleep.

Joshua figured that he had about seven years' worth of sleep to catch up on and a bus rolling down the highway was a better place than many for it.

He didn't sleep well on the nights he ended up

on the bus-depot benches. First of all, they were damned uncomfortable. But he'd spent seven years learning to sleep almost anywhere so that wasn't the real problem.

It was the smell. It took him right back to all the things he was trying to forget. Stale sweat. Poverty. Sorrow. Cheap liquor and even cheaper food. Disease.

It wasn't until he had spent six months in a barracks with a hundred other men that he realized that disease had a smell.

The odd thing was that the odor of disease seemed to vanish in the daytime. Joshua imagined it retreating against the heat and warmth of the sun, but it returned in full force the minute the sun disappeared.

So he couldn't sleep in bus depots. He began to plan his routes, not by destination, but by arrival and departure times. He studied the timetables as if they were battle orders.

And gradually, without noticing it, Joshua made his way to the middle of the country. He felt better where he could see the horizon, where nothing blocked his view of the sky. He no longer craved the smell of the sea, preferring the light sweet scent of the prairie grasses.

He spent another four weeks on short-haul

routes, circling around his quarry, a place where he could feel safe.

Joshua had dreamed of a house in the country, a big sprawling kind of place, with lots of windows and open fields surrounding it. He wanted horses, he thought, though he'd never ridden one, and maybe some goats.

Goats were fascinating animals, their yellow devil's eyes intelligent and aware. He'd met a herd of them in a small village in France where he'd been stationed for several weeks. They ate anything, and that made them perfect animals for the French farmers who'd been making do for years without much at all.

Joshua loved that village. It was the only place he'd felt comfortable in Europe. There was something about it that drew him in, made him relax as he strolled along the narrow streets.

By the time he arrived, weeks behind the big push, the guns had moved on, and the village had mostly been spared. A few crumbling buildings, but most had survived the shelling.

He was billeted into a small stone house on the outskirts of the village. His room looked out over a lush green valley. It had once been fields of grain, but like most of Europe, there was no longer the manpower to seed it.

The house wore a sign, as did most every house in France. Joshua liked that habit, liked the names instead of numbers. This house, his house, was named *Coeurs Mystiques* and Joshua had carefully written it on a scrap of paper and placed it in his duffel.

He'd carried that scrap of paper with him for five years, through battles, hospitals, barracks and sad, divided Berlin. Now, he pulled it from his pocket and read the faded writing one more time: *Coeurs Mystiques*.

Mystic Hearts. He was going to name his house Mystic Hearts. And this was his stop.

He'd been on the bus for three months, circling ever closer to where he wanted to be. This city would be the jumping-off point. He was getting off the bus and he was staying off.

He grabbed his duffel and started walking. He needed a cheap room and an even cheaper car because he was never getting on another bus.

He needed the car because he was going to find his safe place somewhere in the country around this city. He expected it might take some time, but he knew, without any doubt, that Mystic Hearts was nearby.

He found a room in a cheap rooming house right around the corner from the bus depot. It was clean and the landlady served two meals a day. Now he had to buy a car.

The landlady pointed him west.

"The car dealerships are that way," she said. "It's a long way."

Joshua grinned.

"I'll walk it."

He just stepped out into the sunshine and started hoofing it. The pavement sang beneath his feet and he whistled as he walked, some wisp of a melody that he couldn't identify.

Being off the bus was heaven. Being this close to his dream was satisfying.

Joshua wondered how long it would take before he found Mystic Hearts. Today, he'd buy a car and a map, plot out his route. Tomorrow, he'd start searching.

Joshua never did buy a car.

He headed west, the sun warming his back. Ninety minutes later, he had passed from the dingy streets surrounding the bus depot into a street of older well-kept houses along cobblestone streets.

He smiled. The cobbled streets reminded him of France, though nothing else did. No village in France would have these brightly colored and ornate Victorian houses; no village in France would have these exuberant English-cottage gardens.

He felt at home on this street in a way he hadn't felt since France. So he slowed his quick pace and enjoyed the sensation, savoring the peace.

A few people passed him, nodding hello as they did. Several dogs left their yards and sniffed at his pant legs, wagging their tails when he scratched behind their ears. A cat lay on the sidewalk, soaking up the sun, and refused to move at Joshua's passing.

He slowed even further. A wood-and-wrought-iron bench beckoned. He sat, his hands in his lap, and slowly absorbed the change in his circumstances.

He wasn't going to live in the country, he was going to live on this street, in one of these beautiful houses.

Joshua looked across the street at a pale yellow house with white lace curtains on its windows. A For Sale sign swung from a post in the front yard. It had obviously been there for months, maybe years.

The house wore its age with dignity like his father's shoes had always done; slightly worn at the heels, but still polished and cared for.

That was the sign he'd been waiting for. This was the house he had dreamed of.

Coeurs Mystiques.

Mystic Hearts.

CHAPTER 12

That night, snuggled into the white chenille bedspread, Joshua's food in her belly and Marta's first aid soothing her feet, Francesca had trouble getting to sleep. Nothing really new about that, she didn't sleep much anyway, but this time she wasn't able to distract herself with a book or the overnight radio talk shows.

She was stuck inside her own head and she wasn't at all happy about being there.

She contemplated her life, her solitary life. And she wondered whether it wasn't time to change it.

She liked the women she worked with at the coffee shop, enjoyed the odd geeks and nerds who frequented the Internet café in the small hours of the night. She liked seeing the same customers day after day, hearing about their kids and grandkids.

She smiled and chatted with the bus drivers on her regular routes. She knew every one of the kids who worked at the secondhand bookstore she frequented and they knew her by name.

But she never allowed herself to care about any of them. If they weren't there one day, that was just fine by Francesca. She noted their absence and moved on with her life.

Lots of women were single in their forties; few were as single as Francesca.

She had never had a problem finding dates; there were men everywhere. Francesca had figured out long ago that men really liked women who didn't care about relationships.

So she'd had her share of dates over the years, a few of them even lasting long enough to meet Susannah and C.J. Usually, though, they lasted just long enough to get obsessed with Francesca. As soon as she noticed any hint of serious interest, she dumped them. Francesca ensured she was always the dumper, never the dumpee.

She had a list of behaviors that indicated it was time to move on. She had honed this list over many years and she referred to it religiously. The list, printed on bright yellow paper and posted to her refrigerator with a magnet saying Age Doesn't Count Unless You're A Cheese, said that it was time to go if he:

Called more than once a week or called again when his call was not returned right away.

E-mailed more than twice a week.

Signed his e-mails with the word *love*.

Suggested that he meet the family.

Insisted on more than three dates a month.

Brought or sent red roses (tulips and daffodils were okay).

Sent cards of any kind, but especially the kind that came in the mail.

Bought anything that wasn't consumable (books were acceptable, but they had to be paperbacks).

Started to talk about the future. If he said the words *summer vacation* combined with the word *our*, it was over immediately.

The list in Francesca's head was much longer than the list on the fridge, but the magnet would only hold a small piece of paper, so she left it at that.

The other indicators were more subtle. She learned to assess the way a man touched her, the way he looked at her, the way he sounded on the phone.

And it wasn't about lust at all. She enjoyed sex, she just didn't want it to mean anything more than sex.

The magazines she read at her hairdresser's all said that women took sex more seriously than men. Francesca knew the opposite was true. The minute a man had sex, he was committed. Especially if he had sex with someone who didn't want anything more than a casual relationship.

It was as if some deeply buried, atavistic part of his brain knew sex was for procreation and so, if he were having sex with Francesca, there had to be at least the possibility of something longer term. That instinct compelled him to search for a deeper relationship than Francesca was willing to offer him.

He started exhibiting all the behaviors on the list.

And it wasn't as if Francesca were a sex goddess. She was pretty sure she wasn't. She failed all the *How to Please Your Man* quizzes, didn't wear anything except cotton underwear and never wore perfume.

She smelled mostly of rancid fat from the coffee shop with an underlying layer of dusty paper. But that didn't seem to stop them from obsessing over her.

Francesca had given up dating about four years earlier—it was just too much trouble. She'd kept the list, though. It reminded her of why she wasn't dating.

It wasn't simply because of the list, either.

She dumped men for the same reason she didn't want to stay with Joshua and Marta. Francesca wasn't sure she could stand another loss in her life.

But maybe, just maybe, Joshua and Marta were different. She'd spent twenty-four hours with them and in that time they'd insinuated themselves into her psyche in a way no one since Susannah and C.J. in grade five had managed.

So maybe she should stay at Mystic Hearts and see what it was that drew her to that house and those people.

She'd stay and eat chocolate. She'd talk to Joshua and Marta. She'd watch the cats and the kids on the street outside. She'd just hang out.

Because one thing being here had forced Francesca to acknowledge was that she needed to allow other people into her life. She needed to open her heart.

The trouble with doing that was that it might hurt.

Francesca had made two friends. She loved Susannah and C.J. in a way she'd never been able to love her mother. They were the family she chose, and they were her best friends. But she hadn't been at all interested in making any more friends until last night, until she'd realized that she was not only never going to have any new friends, but if she wasn't careful, she'd be losing her old ones.

She put all these worries aside. She'd deal with it some other time, some other day.

She slept right around the clock, which seemed both odd and delicious, going to bed and then also waking up in broad daylight. Francesca couldn't remember the last time she'd done that.

For many years, her life had seemed bound by darkness.

Even in July and August, she went to work in the half light of a summer dawn, came home in the starlit blackness of the night.

Summers were worse than winters.

"I hate getting up in the dark," customers would say in the midst of December and Francesca could agree and feel as if she were a part of the regular world. "It's so depressing going to work *and* coming home in the dark," Neo might say in January and Francesca could nod, feeling normal.

But in the summer, especially coming up to Midsummer eve and the longest day, people would say, "I love coming home and having hours of daylight to play with," or "The sun wakes me up now. I don't even need an alarm clock."

The magic of midsummer didn't work for Francesca. It just depressed her to watch the shorts-and-sunglasses clad crowds enjoy the warm bright evenings.

In winter, she, like almost everyone else, only saw daylight through glass. On sunny days in Decembers and Januarys, she would take a few minutes to stand in the back door of the coffee shop with the smokers, enjoying the sunlight, and wondering what it would be like to live a life where feeling it on your face wasn't quite such a unique experience.

She spent much of her life being scared. Scared because she was always in the dark, traveling back and forth in the licorice-black night. Scared because she might not be able to make the rent at the end of the month and she'd end up as a bag lady. Scared because she had no savings, no pension, no assets. Scared because, like most people in her neighborhood, she was one paycheck away from the street.

And scared because she was alone.

Francesca couldn't shake any of those fears. What she did instead was pretend she wasn't scared.

She filled her days so full she didn't have time to think about what might happen when she had to go home in the dark or pay the rent or buy groceries.

She distracted herself from the stab of dread she felt each time a cashier swiped her bank or credit card by flirting with the male cashiers and chatting with the female ones.

She stayed up until she was so tired; six nights out of seven she fell asleep on the couch or with her head cradled in her arms on the kitchen table.

She conscientiously practiced relaxation exercises so that when she woke up in the middle of the night she could relax herself back to sleep. If that didn't work—and mostly it didn't—she got out of bed and watched late-night television.

She wanted to save for a computer, but knew it was impossible. And even if she somehow, incredibly, figured out a way to buy one, she'd never have the money each month for Internet access, which was what she really needed in the middle of the night.

She took every course she could afford at the Learning Annex. Over the past couple of years she'd taken courses on Chinese cooking, glassblowing, bookbinding, Spanish for travelers (although she'd never been out of the country) and buying stocks, which did seem, even to Francesca, a complete waste of time. She'd taken it anyway.

Francesca had distraction down to a fine art. She rarely, if ever, had time to fret about her life, and that was how she liked it.

But maybe this year would be different.

She wanted to get to know Joshua and Marta, at least she thought she did. At the very least, she thought, she wanted to get rid of her craving for them, for Bains Candies, for her room at the butter-yellow house.

Today was going to be the test.

Her desire to get to know Joshua and Marta

wasn't about Francesca's life, it was about... Well, what was it about?

She wasn't certain, but it was a craving and Francesca had experience with cravings. She knew what to do with them. You indulged them and they went away.

Besides, she was pretty sure that Bains Candies, Joshua, Marta and Mystic Hearts weren't as wonderful as she wanted them to be.

She'd met them after she'd spent an hour in the pouring rain running from three muggers. Her feet were ripped to shreds, her legs were like strands of overcooked spaghetti; she was dripping wet and freezing cold. She was scared to death.

Almost anywhere would have felt like heaven in those circumstances.

CHAPTER 13

Marta smiled at Joshua as he fidgeted around the shop. The CLOSED sign had been replaced by the OPEN one almost an hour earlier. He'd opened the shop for the early morning breakfast crowd but closed it as soon as he heard Francesca moving around upstairs.

Now he was polishing the glass cases, rearranging the chocolates, straightening his tie and checking his reflection in the mirror behind the kitchen door.

Joshua seemed certain that Francesca was going to stay at Mystic Hearts. Marta was less sure, but she'd pretended not to be so for Joshua's sake.

She drank her first cup of coffee and then hurried upstairs to hover outside Francesca's room. Joshua went down to the kitchen to bake fresh bread and put a pot roast in the slow cooker.

"She'll stay," Joshua repeated over and over again, as if by saying it he would ensure its truth.

Marta nodded in response. But she knew convincing Francesca to accept help wasn't going to be easy. She was as stubborn and as independent as Joshua.

It had taken Joshua a year to accept Marta's help and, even at the end of that year, he would have refused her help if she'd given him the chance. In the end, she made the decision for him and simply stayed, daring him to toss her out.

That tactic wasn't going to work on Francesca but Marta had some ideas.

"Joshua," she rasped. "Just invite her to stay to dinner, okay? Don't push her to stay forever. You'll scare her."

Marta's voice vanished beneath a storm of coughing. She doubled over and tried to force breath through her throat. Patient, she had to be patient. She wasn't going to suffocate. Joshua wouldn't let it happen.

Sweat poured from her face as the coughs racked her small frame.

"Marta?" Joshua rubbed her back, the one thing almost certain to soothe her coughing. "Relax, beautiful. Just relax."

His voice wrapped itself around her allowing her to calm just enough so that air could get through the constricted passage.

"I'll ask her to stay for dinner. I'll tell her stories about making candy. I won't even mention forever."

Marta had finally managed to breathe in enough air that she no longer felt in danger of collapsing. She nodded and tried a small smile.

She gestured at her throat and shook her head.

"No more talking for you today," Joshua replied to her gestures. "It's a bad day, isn't it?"

Marta mouthed *yes*, and pantomimed pushing the vacuum.

"I get it. You can't talk because you did too much housework?"

She grinned.

"Uh-uh. Nice try, beautiful, but I've seen you do the spring cleaning around here. Plus I've seen you shift ten yards of soil in a day."

Joshua kept rubbing her back, slowly moving up and down her spine, his big hands spanning her back from shoulder to shoulder.

"Stress," she whispered.

"Me, too," he said, resting his forehead against hers. "Me, too."

Marta took his hands from her shoulders and held them at her chest. She turned them over and kissed his palms, one after the other, remembering the hundreds of times he'd used those hands to soothe her.

Marta had always been drawn to hands and she'd often chosen her lovers because of their hands. Pianists and conductors and painters. They all had beautiful hands, but despite their beauty, not one of them could compete with Joshua.

His hands, all knobbly and worn, somehow managed to be the most sensual, soft, soothing hands in the world. Marta wished that Rembrandt could come back from the dead just long enough to paint Joshua's hands. They were the hands of a saint and a sinner, a working man and an aesthete.

Joshua pushed Marta farther into the shop, patting her bum as he did so.

"You sit down," he said. "I'll watch for her. She should be down any minute."

Marta didn't question his certainty. She also felt Francesca's presence growing stronger. Her heart began to race. So much depended on this morning, not just for her and Joshua, but also for Francesca. She needed it to go well.

Waiting might kill Joshua.

She'd watched him get thinner over the past few months. He wasn't sleeping, either. He pretended to sleep, keeping his body motionless in the bed, but Joshua was a restless sleeper and Marta had learned to roll with him as he moved through the night.

The stillness gave him away. Marta didn't say a

word about it, letting his pretence stand, ignoring his lack of hunger, his red-rimmed eyes and sad face.

Making candy was Joshua's job, saving souls was his life. Failure was his biggest fear.

Over the years, Joshua had told her the story of almost every Midsummer eve.

"I've told you about every person I can remember," he'd said to her about ten years earlier. But once every couple of years, something would remind him of another Midsummer eve and they'd spend the next few nights sitting up in bed, candles on the bedside table instead of the harsher electric light, a bottle of wine and two glasses next to the candles.

Joshua always began the story with the exact same words.

"It was midnight."

He never referred to it as Midsummer eve, that was Marta's take. It had taken her a fair few stories before she had realized that each story took place on the same night. She pointed this out to Joshua.

He shrugged.

"I don't think that means anything," he said and insisted on using the date.

"It was a dark night, raining and cold."

The first sentence never changed.

Marta could always tell how the story would begin, not exactly how, but how terribly, by Joshua's face. This story began with tears standing stark in his eyes.

Henry Finder (Joshua remembered every name) was the saddest man he'd ever met. His entire family—his wife and three children, both sets of grandparents, two aunts, three uncles and four cousins—were killed in a fire one late summer evening while he was at work. To make it even worse, he was a fireman. The fire had been randomly set by an arsonist but he had got it in his mind that the fire was his fault.

He had been off work for weeks, drinking heavily, and taking the worst kind of chances with his life. He wanted to kill himself, but he was Catholic and he couldn't bear to add the guilt of suicide to his already guilt-ridden mind.

He became a kind of vigilante, prowling the mean streets of the worst part of the city, watching for anyone who might be carrying the ingredients needed to torch a house or a business.

The arsonist who had killed his family had not been found and the police had few clues. Henry wanted, more than anything, to find and punish the arsonist. Once that happened, he believed that he could simply lie down, stop eating and drink himself to death. But until then, he ate just enough to keep himself alive, drank enough so he could pass out for a few hours each night and spent every other moment on the streets.

He told Joshua early on that he didn't carry a gun. He wanted to kill the man with his bare hands; a gun, he felt, would be too impersonal.

The year before had been the first time Joshua had truly considered what Mystic Hearts was doing. Joshua had lived in the house for almost five years before his mind was able to absorb it. Up until then, Joshua thought of these damaged souls arriving at his door as a coincidence. He hadn't even realized until Henry Finder that every one of them had arrived at Mystic Hearts at precisely the same time on the same night of the year.

This year, for the first time, Joshua was expecting someone. There was no neon light back then, but somehow people still found their way down that dark alley to the door.

He appeared, sprawling across the doorstep, dazed and more confused than anyone before him.

He had been running, he told Joshua over a cup of hot chocolate, chasing evil through the darkness. He had been close to catching this man when he'd stumbled over the stoop in front of the shop.

He wasn't sure that it was *his* arsonist, or even that the man had done anything wrong, but it hadn't seemed to matter to him at the time. He had spotted him standing under a street lamp, his blond hair gleaming in the light, a cigarette in his mouth, and Henry had snapped.

This man was evil. He felt it, he said, felt it through to the very marrow of his bones. He had not a single doubt that if he killed the blond man, he would be doing the world a favor. He walked up to the man, asked to borrow a light, and then, when the man was reaching into his pocket for a match, he hit him.

He smashed at his face with a rage that was unquenchable. He pounded at him even after he fell to the ground, even after blood started to pool under his head, from his nose, from his mouth.

Once the man was down, Henry Finder kicked him in the ribs, in the kidneys, in the knee. He felt at least one rib break and maybe another bone in his right leg.

He would have killed the blond man, Henry told Joshua, but something scared him. It would have taken the devil himself to scare him that night, he said, but something did. Something scared him enough to stop him from killing that man.

Henry never did know what it was that had scared

him, only that it had started him running, racing away from the fear until he stumbled over the front stoop.

Joshua settled Henry into the room upstairs and walked out into the rain to find the blond man, hoping it wasn't too late to help him and deliver him to a hospital.

He was gone.

Joshua made the rounds of the hospitals and the morgue, but there was no sign of a badly beaten blond man. For days after, he checked the papers, listened to the radio news, trolled for gossip. The man had vanished. It was as if he'd never existed.

Henry's sorrow and his pain turned a cold into pneumonia and he spent the next few weeks hovering on the brink. He drifted in and out of consciousness until, one day, almost four weeks later, he shook off the delirium and woke up.

He asked first about the blond man. "I was unable to find any sign of him," Joshua said, and Henry laughed a little at that.

"He was an angel," Henry said. "That blond man had to be an angel. He'd be dead," Henry said, "if he wasn't."

"An angel?" Joshua asked. "Are you sure?" He didn't ask what had made him savage an angel.

"That angel knew I would never move on, knew

that I needed a catalyst, so he made himself into one. He forced me to spew out all the hatred and rage I'd been feeling and then he brought me to this place."

Henry Finder looked around the room, at the faded wallpaper and the gilt-framed pictures. "This room," he said, "this room brought me the peace I needed to decide what to do with the rest of my life."

Now, at the time, Henry couldn't have been more than twenty-seven or twenty-eight, but when he said those words to Joshua, he had the confidence and serenity of a man fifty years older.

"I'm going to the seminary," he said, "and I'm going to become a priest. I'm going to tell people about my miracle, and I'm going to tell them that sometimes something good comes from the most evil of acts."

"Henry's gone now, though every few summers he drops by for a day," Joshua said. He'd been gone for a very long time, but Joshua knew he still told the story of his miracle, and he still swore that the blond man was an angel.

Joshua always smiled at the end of that story. He smiled at the end of every story, even when he told of people who hadn't lived through their tales.

Marta kept a list of the stories Joshua told, not writing down the entire story—they were far too long for that—but a few pages, just enough to remind her of each one.

She included the stories she had been a part of, bringing the total number on her list up to fifty-four. Twenty damaged souls and twenty stories since she had been at Mystic Hearts (including herself) and thirty-four from the years before her arrival.

Joshua had been successful with every person, at least every person he chose to remember. In the last few years, once she'd realized that she wasn't going to end up with sixty people on her list, Marta had more than occasionally wondered whether the missing stories had been failures. She had never dared ask.

Joshua's voice pulled her from her memories.

"She's coming downstairs," he said, impatiently shifting from one foot to the other.

Good, Marta said to herself. *It's about time*.

CHAPTER 14

Nothing had changed at Bains Candies except for the OPEN sign on the front door. Francesca frowned at it as she reached the bottom of the stairs, frowned at the strangers sitting at *her* table.

Her decision to stay and get to know Joshua and Marta shattered at the sight of Joshua smiling at the couple sitting at *her* table. His smile, Marta's care—they weren't about her. They cared about everyone.

The solitude and fear she'd managed to shunt to one side crashed down on her. She was out of here. Francesca could cope with her life in familiar surroundings; she'd done it forever.

But this storybook place just made her realize how sad and lonely she really was. She waved at Joshua and limped for the door. No more goodbyes.

Marta watched Francesca from the kitchen. She was leaving, that was no surprise; what was surprising was Joshua. He smiled at Francesca and waved back before turning to Marta.

"It'll be all right," he said. "Don't worry. She'll be back."

Marta shook her head in puzzlement. Joshua obviously knew more than she did because she'd been watching the stairs all morning, waiting for Francesca to creep down them and sneak out the door. And she didn't expect her to come back.

And she had left. Okay, she hadn't quite sneaked, but she had left. But Joshua didn't look worried, not the way he had yesterday, so Marta was going to leave it be.

Francesca limped out onto the street and tried not to think of how Joshua had smiled and waved goodbye as if he didn't care she was leaving. She was leaving and she didn't care either. But she did need a coffee to keep her company as she walked the few blocks to the bus. A small coffee shop waited for her at the corner. Not as nice as Bains, but still fine.

She didn't know how to get home, but she knew it wasn't too far. She would start at the coffee shop and walk a few blocks in any direction. If it started getting colder, if the streets lost their sparkle, she would know she was heading in the right direction. If not, she'd turn back, retrace her steps and start again in another direction.

She'd just keep doing that until she walked out of enchantment and into reality.

Extra-large coffee securely in hand, she turned away from Mystic Hearts. And stopped, her feet suddenly mired in invisible sand. The coffee cup jerked from Francesca's hand and she almost followed it the ground.

Francesca picked up her now empty cup from the street and turned around to go back to the coffee shop to replace it. The feeling of pressure on her shoulders and legs disappeared, until she replaced her coffee and started walking away from Bains Candies.

She stopped in the middle of the sidewalk, then turned around and took a few steps toward Mystic Hearts. She moved as easily as if she were a fish in water.

She stopped again and spun around. She took a step, then another. She might have been wearing ten-pound weights around each ankle.

She turned again. The weights were gone.

Francesca stopped dead, her feet in what she thought of as neutral, facing neither toward nor away from Mystic Hearts. She turned her head left, then right. The head turn worked fine.

She shifted her shoulders, first one way, then the other. That, too, caused no problems. Both directions seemed the same.

Her hips were next. She knew she looked like an

idiot, but she didn't care. She needed to figure this out. She twisted right, then left, then did it again. Nothing.

Maybe she had imagined it. Of course she had imagined it. Francesca laughed self-consciously.

"I'm an idiot," she said, then looked around quickly to make sure no one was around to hear her speak.

She shifted left and headed for the coffee shop. It was like walking in fine deep sand on a humid August afternoon. It was painful. And extremely familiar.

She'd been fighting whatever it was for… She wasn't sure how long the fight had been going on, but she was certain that she'd recognized it when she headed back toward Mystic Hearts. And she recognized it because it was gone.

Well, Francesca Bond wasn't going to let a little invisible sand keep her from her coffee. She slogged the half block to the coffee shop and bought *another* extra-large coffee, with triple cream and five packets of brown sugar.

This time, the sand reappeared the minute she started walking away from Mystic Hearts. She stopped and turned her face toward the candy store. The pause allowed her just enough time for reality to sink in.

"Shit. Shit, shit, shit."

She whispered the words under her breath, her hands shaking with fear.

This couldn't be good, she thought. She hesitated at the corner until the light turned red again.

Should she turn back? Because whatever was going on, it was connected to that house, and it was scaring the bejesus out of her.

Francesca's heart raced. She felt her face redden and her legs start to shake. Hot coffee spilled over her hand as the shakes progressed into her fingers. She dropped her second cup of coffee.

"Sit down," she whispered. "Sit down right now."

She sat on the curb and started her most effective relaxation exercise.

Breathe in for ten.

Hold for ten.

Breathe out for ten.

Repeat as necessary.

Five sets later, and she was barely calm enough to realize that it wasn't going to work. She needed something stronger.

Pinch right nostril.

Breathe in left nostril.

Pinch left nostril.

Breath out right nostril.

Repeat as necessary.

The shaking had slowed to a manageable level and Francesca lifted herself from the curb.

She looked down at the coffee spilled in the gutter, picked up the cup and dropped it in the garbage at the corner. Now she needed a coffee more than ever.

She turned back and determinedly pushed her way through the sand to the coffee shop.

"Large Americano, triple cream, right?" The young man behind the counter remembered her.

Of course he remembered her. She'd ordered three coffees in the space of half an hour. He must think she was severely hungover. She cleared her throat.

"Yes, please," she said and held out her still shaking hand with the money in it.

"You okay, lady?"

"I'm fine."

"Listen," he said, handing her the cup, "have this one on me."

She smiled at him and hurried out of the shop. While she'd been waiting for the coffee, she'd made up her mind. Whatever the weird craving thing was, wherever it was coming from, she was going to have to deal with it.

Distraction was not going to work. Now that she'd experimented enough with the craving to know her boundaries, she could no longer ignore it.

She wanted to get the whole thing over with so

she could go back to her old life. The past half hour had convinced her that her second plan for the summer was a lousy one. Getting to know Joshua and Marta was a bad idea and she was going back to Bains Candies to tell them so.

She marched toward Joshua and Marta, hurrying down the block, her strides free and her anger mounting.

She tried to ignore the tiny hints of pink or flashes of yellow, unidentifiable, then bushes of fuschia and red and golden rhododendrons. Pale lavender wisteria overhung porches and roses of every color sang in the heat. It was a fairy tale made real.

Francesca expected to see Shakespeare's Titania, Peaseblossom and Mustardseed cavorting among the blossoms waiting for Puck's arrival. The gardens were out of fairy tales or storybooks, and the scents?

The sweetness lay in the air, deep and rich and heady. Each breath made her dizzy.

A million shades of green tinted the sidewalks, the fences and the houses.

Bumblebees buzzed, burying themselves in the summer abundance.

Francesca walked through the glory in a daze. She had long since finished her coffee; her keys and the change from the coffees were in her pocket, so her hands were free to caress the blossoms.

Her pace slowed almost to a standstill as she neared the house. She would go in even though it scared her to death.

She was going to go in. Soon. Really. She was going to open that door, come hell or high water.

She sat down on the top step and looked over her shoulder at the sign and then up at the face of the house.

Where was the red neon? And the alley?

Francesca had spent much of the past two days trying to figure out how so much had changed between that night and the morning after.

She had no trouble enumerating what had changed. The house had somehow moved from a dark alley to a brilliantly sunny street. The red neon that had attracted her in the first place was replaced by a copperplate sign saying Bains Candies.

The neighborhoods could not possibly be the same. The frightening gloomy streets she'd raced through in the rain did not, could not, connect with the cobblestoned streets she saw the next morning.

Francesca looked up at the house, tracing the few wires that ran from the telephone poles to the house. She looked for signs, even turned-off signs, but there was nothing.

There was no neon.

She slumped over her knees and waited. She watched the shadows creep across the sidewalk.

"When the shadows hit the curb, I'm going in," she said to her knees.

The shadows curled over the curb and Francesca changed her refrain.

"When the shadows cover the bush at the corner, I'm going in."

This time, though, she didn't wait.

Her patience was exhausted. She stood back up and contemplated the door. Should she stay or should she go? The sand was definitely a factor in the decision-making process.

Still, she thought, *maybe now that I'm here the sand has swept itself back to where it came from*. She stepped down onto the first stair to the street.

The sand wasn't gone; it had piled up even deeper. She could barely move through it now. The sand had turned to quicksand and with each step she was sinking deeper into it.

She pulled herself backward up the steps and leaned, gasping for breath, against the door.

Bang. Bang. Bang.

Francesca hammered on the glass, practically falling into Joshua's arms when the door flew open.

"Francesca," he said, helping her to the table where Marta waited. "We're so glad you're back."

Francesca caught an odd glance streaking from Marta to Joshua, part joy, part warning. She couldn't decipher it, but it was obvious that it was about her.

"Can you stay for dinner? I made pot roast. I know it's warm but almost everyone likes pot roast. I baked bread, too. Can you smell it? There's nothing like fresh baked bread. And I got both salted and unsalted butter. I wasn't sure what you liked. I didn't make lunch, but there's honey ham and cheddar in the fridge, and I made some rolls yesterday. I didn't know what kind of desserts you liked, but I remembered you drank hot chocolate and you can never go wrong with chocolate so I baked a chocolate cake and made some chocolate-chip cookies."

"Ah-hem," Marta cleared her throat and threw another look at Joshua, this one containing less joy and much more warning.

"Would you like a cup of tea or something, Francesca?" Joshua somehow managed to stop himself after the one sentence.

"I'd love a cup of coffee."

"I'll just go make a fresh pot." And Joshua rushed away, pushing through the swinging doors to the kitchen.

"He's excited," Marta whispered. "Just ignore

him for a little bit and he'll calm down when he sees that you're not going to leave right away. You're not, are you?"

"No."

Francesca had no idea what to say after that. She had spent the hours on the street practicing a speech, which had now basically disappeared, lost somewhere in the fog of her overwhelmed brain.

She remembered, vaguely, what the speech had been about. She'd planned to ask all the questions buzzing in her head. How had Joshua known she was coming? How had she been able to imagine the room at the top of the stairs so perfectly before she'd even seen it? How had the house moved? Was this really the House?

Francesca wanted answers to all those questions but the urgency seemed to have dissipated once she'd returned to Mystic Hearts.

That was another question she wanted answered. Why was the house called Mystic Hearts? And how did she know that?

But none of the questions seemed important now she was here.

What Francesca really wanted, and it seemed perfectly clear now she'd arrived, was to go upstairs to the room at the top of the stairs and make sure that nothing had changed.

Marta must have read her mind.

"Why don't you go upstairs and freshen up," she said. "Your room's waiting."

"But Joshua..."

"The coffeepot's an old one, it will take him a while to finish making the coffee. Take your time, Francesca."

CHAPTER 15

Marta wanted Francesca to go upstairs. Joshua needed another pep talk.

The kitchen, as always, smelled wonderful. Today it smelled mostly of the bread Joshua had baked this morning, but it also retained a faint hint of caramel and cinnamon.

Marta stood at the open door and looked out over her garden. The birds were singing and she couldn't help herself; she was drawn out to join them.

The garden was her pride and joy. She had spent twenty years tilling its soil, dark and rich and pungent. The best part of her day was spent planting, tending it, finding the plants the birds loved, the colors that attracted bees, the softest, greenest grass. The garden was hers in a way the house would never be.

Oh, she loved Mystic Hearts, just as she loved Joshua. But she'd built the garden. It was her place.

She sat on the steps and started humming.

A small covered pail stood on the top step and she reached for it without turning her head. She grabbed a handful of grain and continued to hum, mimicking the various songs in the garden, merging them into a whole, a symphony.

A tiny black-capped chickadee spiraled down and landed on her palm, picking delicately at the grain. She hummed at him and waited.

A larger brown wren joined the chickadee. Her weight overbalanced Marta's hand and the chickadee started to slide off. Marta dropped her hand to her knee and kept up the humming. The two birds sang while they ate the grain, Marta's humming pulling the two disparate voices together, like the cello in a string quartet.

A robin, much bigger and heavier, spun down for a look, hesitated, and then landed on Marta's knee. Its voice added a deeper tone to the concert.

Finally, a shy bluebird joined them and Marta's day was complete. The bluebird was her lucky bird—she'd loved them since she was a child and had read the fairy tales about the bluebird of happiness—and its appearance meant the day would go well.

Marta smiled to herself. It wasn't going to be an easy day, she had seen that in Francesca's face, but now that she knew it was going to work out, she would be able to steer Joshua and Francesca into a détente.

"Joshua," she said, coming back through the door into the kitchen, "we need to talk."

She touched Joshua's shoulder and turned him away from his contemplation of the coffeepot.

"I know, I know," he said, "a watched pot never boils."

She rested her head on his chest and smiled into his sweater.

"Hmmm," she hummed into his heart, just as she'd hummed to the birds, this time at a lower pitch.

"That feels good. I think it makes the ache go away."

She hummed, louder now to drown out the sorrow that overwhelmed her whenever she thought about Joshua's heart.

Perhaps, Marta thought, she could give him the peace he had given her. He wanted, more than anything, someone to take over Mystic Hearts. He was convinced that someone was Francesca.

"She's scared, Joshua," Marta whispered.

"I know, and I'm making it worse, aren't I?"

Marta nodded.

"I can't seem to help myself."

Marta lifted her head from his chest and grinned at him.

"So what's new, right? It's important. She's the right one, Marta, and I don't have much time."

Marta's tears spilled onto Joshua's sweater, a small pool of dampness that somehow managed to penetrate the sweater and the shirt under it and go directly to Joshua's heart like a spear composed wholly of love.

Francesca stood in the kitchen doorway.

She looked carefully at Joshua and Marta, wondering what it was that had brought two such disparate human beings together. It was obvious they loved each other but not at all in the way Francesca would have expected.

She expected people of Joshua's age to be content with their lives, to have given up the passionate feelings of youth. But Joshua's passion for Marta was clear in his face, in the timbre of his voice.

Eighty years old and he still managed to retain the fever of a young man for his woman. He stood tall and thin next to Marta. He watched over her as if she were the most precious thing in the world, and she did the same for him.

Marta's face was beautiful, but she took no care

to hide her ravaged throat or her ruined voice. She, too, carried hidden passion. But she was also tender.

The way her arms wrapped around Joshua, the way she kissed each part of his face, the way she pushed the hair off his forehead. These movements were as tender as a mother with her child.

The passion blazed when she touched his lips. She looked as if she had gone up in flames before him.

Francesca backed away from the kitchen door, stepped silently back across the tiled floor in the shop and halted at the bottom of the stairs. She found herself drawn to that passion despite her fear of it.

She took a deep breath and then clomped across the tiled floors.

"Joshua? Marta? Where are you?"

This time, when she reached the kitchen door, the two of them were standing at the sink, hand in hand, passion now banked.

Francesca heard a sound that reminded her of the beautiful day waiting outside the house. It made her want to take off her shoes and walk barefoot in the grass at dawn. It made her feel the dew on her feet while she savored the warmth of the sun on her shoulders.

Marta was humming, her voice low and sweet and perfect.

The humming came from deep in Marta's chest. Francesca couldn't figure out how that flawless sound came through that ravaged throat but she didn't want it to stop.

"Marta?"

The humming stopped and Francesca felt a loss so deep and painful that she almost dropped to the floor.

A large warm hand reached to hold her up.

"Don't worry," Joshua said. "She hums most of the day. Wait until you see how the birds sing back to her."

Francesca grabbed Joshua's hand and let him pull her to her feet.

"Let's have some coffee and some scones," he said. "I bet you're hungry. I am."

A faint reminder of the passion she'd witnessed flashed through his eyes and then disappeared behind an equally fascinating veil of kindness.

Francesca sat at the little round table in the shop and tried to take in everything that had happened to her that morning. It was impossible.

She felt a little like Alice, trying to believe ten impossible things before breakfast.

From the moment she'd walked out the front door and identified the sand trap, she had been faced with one impossible thing after another. Francesca was getting tired of it, damn tired. *Come hell or high water*, she thought, *come hell or high water*. She recited the words to herself, counting on them to anchor her in this world.

Because Francesca was pretty sure Joshua and Marta lived in another, far better world. It was a world that had nothing in common with her world. The sad part was that she preferred Mystic Hearts.

Who wouldn't?

Francesca lived in a one-room apartment. It was clean and it was tidy. She had her books and her posters, but her windows looked out over an alley filled with pain.

Francesca needed her room to be a refuge and occasionally, in the middle of a Sunday afternoon or the darkest part of the night once everyone slept and before they woke, it was. But mostly the world outside was too close, too noisy, too dangerous and too sad.

Every morning, she woke to the sound of men rifling through the bins in the alley, looking for bottles and cans to trade in for a meal unless they found leftovers to feed themselves, in which case the bottles and cans were traded in for smokes or cheap alcohol.

By the end of the day, the alley glittered with used needles, burned spoons and broken bottles. A van cruised through a couple of times a day, carrying nurses from the needle exchange.

People worked in shops with grungy windows, served cups of cheap coffee and tea, made hundreds of plates of eggs and toast. Very little bacon got served in Francesca's neighborhood.

The front of her apartment building looked out over a slightly better neighborhood. The street was clean compared to the alley and the office blocks were filled with bookkeepers and tax preparers and process servers.

Her coffee shop was five blocks over and it served a great deal of bacon. Also scones and even the occasional latte. Francesca aspired to live closer to work, but so far she hadn't been able to manage first and last months' rent for a new and better apartment.

She could probably have afforded the rent, but saving a whole extra month's worth was pretty much impossible. So she lived in her one-room apartment with the curtains closed so she didn't have to see the alley.

But here, at Mystic Hearts, Francesca knew she would never close the curtains. She would want to see the street all the time, through all the seasons.

Of course she wanted to move to this street.

But more than that, she wanted her room, with the books and the sheepskin rug and the faded floral wallpaper. She wanted her bathroom with the deep green towels and the claw-footed bathtub.

CHAPTER 16

Francesca relaxed into her chair while Joshua and Marta bustled about, pouring coffee, filling the table with plates and scones and pure white bowls of creamy yellow butter.

She reached out to stop Marta as she dropped a plate of brownies in the middle of the table and turned to race back to the kitchen.

"Marta, sit down, please. That's enough. We can't eat all of this, not just the three of us."

Marta shrugged off Francesca's restraining hand and smiled.

"It can go in the fridge for snacks later."

She hurried back to the kitchen, leaving Francesca in a state of bewilderment.

Kids? Do Joshua and Marta have kids? Is that why they seem so exuberant today?

And then, feeling spiteful and mean, she found herself hoping that they didn't have children, that they had no family, and that they wanted her. They wanted her to live in this house, and she wanted them. And the room.

She cringed at the thought.

I don't want a family, especially an old family.

"We're not really that old, you know," Joshua said, hauling another chair up to the table.

"Can you both..." Francesca didn't say it.

"Sort of. Marta more than me. She has great empathy. I just read people's faces. And you had that look on yours."

"What look?"

"That look so many people get on their face when they see an old person on the street. It's a combination really. A little fear—they don't want to end up all wrinkled and worn and lame. A little thankfulness—they're not old at all. A little disgust—what's an old biddy like that doing on *my* street?

"Once you've seen it directed at you a few times, you get to recognize it."

"I didn't mean..." Francesca mumbled because she had meant it.

"It doesn't matter, love. I *am* old. And some days, I feel that age. Eighty years is a long time to be on this planet."

He poured a cup of coffee, added in a big dollop of thick cream and five teaspoons of brown sugar, and passed it to Francesca.

"Do you want a cup of coffee, my love?"

Marta nodded. He poured another cup of coffee, this one black, and handed it to Marta. His was black with even more sugar than Francesca's.

The three of them sipped their coffee without speaking.

Francesca worked on an icebreaker in her mind but she couldn't get past the questions she hadn't been able to ask. She opened her mouth a couple of times but nothing came out. She was struck dumb.

"Have a scone," Marta said.

"I don't want a scone. I want answers."

"And you'll get them, but there's no need to starve while you're listening, is there?"

Francesca pouted and placed a blueberry scone on her plate. Joshua handed her the butter and a knife.

"Thanks," she said, though thanks were as far from her feelings as could be imagined.

"Francesca," Joshua began once everyone's mouth was full. "We need to ask you a favor."

Marta nodded in support and placed one hand on Joshua's arm, the other on Francesca's.

"A favor? What could I possibly do for you?"

"We need someone to help us at the shop. We can't manage it anymore."

"I'm not a cook." Francesca said the first thing that came to mind, which wasn't the answer she wanted to give, though she wasn't sure what that answer was.

She tried again.

"I like my jobs," she said. "And this is too far for me to come every day."

That was closer, she thought, and more accurate.

And besides, she wasn't ready to give up on the other world, on Susannah and C.J., on her mother, on Neo and Holy Joe, on her regulars at the coffee shop.

She knew, without having to think about it, that saying yes to Joshua's offer would change her life in more ways than she could imagine. She would gain this beautiful, safe place, Joshua and Marta, maybe even surcease from fear, but what would she lose?

"What about my friends? My family?"

Francesca could barely get that question out of her mouth, she could barely even think about it. If she tried, it made not just her head ache, but her entire body. She held her breath, watching Joshua's face, waiting for an answer.

"You can write them," he said, "tell them you're here." He looked over at Marta. "Phone them, as well."

"Can I see them?"

He shrugged.

"I don't know. Maybe."

"No one's ever tried?"

"No one's ever tried during their year, the year they spend at Mystic Hearts getting well. But you, Francesca, you're different. So I don't know the answer to that question."

Shivers ran up Francesca's arms. This was getting too complicated, too scary.

"I'm going home."

"Marta?" Joshua's voice cracked when he spoke Marta's name.

"Francesca." Marta's voice was low and rough as she took over the conversation. "We need your help. We can't do this on our own anymore and we have no family. Could you stay for a while, maybe a few months?"

She coughed, her face turning red with the effort. Without speaking, Francesca handed her a glass of water.

"Please?"

Marta stopped herself from saying that Francesca needed them at least as much as they needed her. She needed Mystic Hearts; she needed a family. But she knew Francesca would react badly to that statement. Her stubborn independence was as obvious as her fear.

"I can write?"

"Yes."

"Phone?"

"Yes."

"Can they come here?"

Marta glanced over at Joshua and he shrugged.

"We don't know. We hope so."

"Can they try?"

Joshua smiled and reached across the table for Francesca's hands.

"Of course they can, though it may only work on Midsummer eve. Or it may not work for the first year. We just don't know, we've never had this situation before."

Francesca considered that for a moment, her hands warm and safe in Joshua's.

"Can I leave if I want to?"

"I think so. I'm pretty sure if you do leave you can't come back. Not ever."

Marta added, "But everything might change at the end of the year, next Midsummer eve. Henry sometimes comes to visit us on that day. I think we'll just have to wait and see."

The three of them sat in silence, waiting for Francesca's decision.

"I'll stay," she finally said. "I'll stay for today and tonight and I'll think about it. I'll phone my jobs and I'll phone Susannah and I'll think about it."

"Your room is upstairs waiting for you," Joshua said.

Marta chimed in, "Joshua likes to cook and the two of us don't eat much. Cooking for you—" she shared a smile with Joshua "—would bring him great pleasure."

I'll be safe, Francesca thought, *on this street*.

Francesca shook her head to clear it of that consideration. Safety wasn't about location. Safety was all about being prepared. And Francesca didn't seem to be able to get prepared. She took lessons with C.J., she carried a can of pepper spray and a cell phone with an automatic emergency dial feature although there was no service at Bains Candies or on the street outside it. She'd tried.

She walked as C.J. had taught her, with a heavy focused stride that said, *This woman knows where she's going*. She worked on feeling in control.

But none of it changed a thing.

Because Francesca wasn't in control. She spent her energy working on not losing what little control she did have, and the rest of it on spiraling out of control.

Moving to this house, this sanctuary, would not help Francesca. It would only make things worse.

CHAPTER 17

Red and blue lights. Flashing. The deep throaty hum of the fire engines waiting impatiently for their occupants to return. Excited voices echoing through the street. And Marta standing in the doorway, wringing her hands.

"Marta," Francesca called, running down the stairs, still half-asleep from her afternoon nap. She had come upstairs to write letters and make phone calls but instead had fallen asleep. The noise of the heavy diesel engines had woken her. "Marta."

"Francesca. I have to go to the hospital to be with Joshua. Here are the keys."

Marta handed Francesca a solid black ring with a few old-fashioned keys attached to it.

"This is the shop door. This one is the kitchen door," she told Francesca, twisting the keys around on the ring.

"Marta. Stop. What's wrong with Joshua?"

Francesca held the hands with the key ring in them and waited.

"Marta? Is he..."

"He had another heart attack. He's going to be okay, they say, but he has to spend a few days in the hospital."

Francesca and Marta watched the ambulance pull away. It didn't have the lights flashing or the sirens blaring. If Joshua had been in real danger, they would have. The fire trucks pulled out behind the ambulance, leaving the street once again silent. Even the excited neighbors had all gone back indoors.

Marta scrambled into the cab at the curb and Francesca was left behind, holding the keys to Mystic Hearts. She had no idea what to do with them.

She made sure the sign on the front door was set to CLOSED. She didn't need any customers, not until she figured out what she needed to do.

Sitting at the table by the window, Francesca looked out at the darkening twilight. She waited for the red neon, wondering if it was so carefully disguised that it was impossible to see except in the dark.

No red neon. No flashing lights.

It obsessed her. She searched the main floor, turning every light switch she saw. On and then off. Still no red neon. She opened the single closed door on the main floor, saw a steep flight of stairs leading down.

She turned all three switches at the head of the basement stairs first on and then off. Still no red neon, although she caught a glimpse of a spotlessly clean basement lined with shelves and shelves of preserves.

She stood at the bottom of the stairs leading up to the bedrooms. She wasn't at all comfortable about going into Joshua and Marta's room but it had to be done. She found an old leather suitcase in a closet in the front hallway and hauled it with her up the stairs.

She opened the door in the middle of the hallway onto a huge room, so big Francesca wondered how they'd built it under such a sloped roof.

Francesca threw sweaters and pants and underwear in the suitcase for Marta. She added the books from each bedside table. A well-read copy of *Watership Down* on one side and a brand new hardcover mystery from the other.

From the bathroom she took toothbrushes, toothpaste, and all the lotions and creams she could find.

The shop and kitchen seemed unbearably quiet

without Joshua and Marta, so Francesca scurried around cleaning up. She cleared the table, washed the dishes, took the pot roast from the slow cooker, wrapped it and put it in the fridge.

She wasn't hungry but she forced herself to eat a couple of slices of Joshua's bread, trying not to think of him lying in a hospital room, wired to all those machines.

She tried not to think of Marta either. Her sorrow had been palpable, weighing her down as she'd walked to the cab. Francesca wasn't sure Marta would survive without Joshua. So much of her strength seemed to come from him, from his certainty and spirit.

But Francesca believed the opposite was also true. Joshua might be eighty, but he didn't act that way at all. She thought back to the scene she'd witnessed in the kitchen and wished, just once, that someone would feel about her the way Joshua and Marta felt about each other.

She sighed and went around the house, checking the doors and the windows. The neighborhood looked safe, but Francesca wasn't willing to take a chance on it. Safety wasn't at all about appearances.

She piled a tray with tea and honey and the few scones they hadn't eaten, turned off the downstairs lights and hurried up the stairs.

The light in her room was on, a warm soft glow on the bed and the sheepskin rug. She locked the door and sat down in the rocking chair to make a list.

She had a million things to do and three at least had to be done right away. She only hoped Joshua had been right and that she could phone from this place—wherever it was—to her old world. She couldn't leave people hanging.

She called the coffee shop.

It wasn't an easy story to tell, mostly because Francesca hadn't had time to think out a very convincing one, but the fact that she started crying when she talked about Joshua leaving in the ambulance did add a bit to the verisimilitude.

"Don't worry, darlin'," the manager said. "You take as much time as you need. Catherine can fill in for you for a while. Her dear old mom's in town and the two of them don't get along. Keep in touch, okay?"

One down, two more to go.

"Neo?"

Everyone at the Internet café had aliases except for Francesca. They'd tried to give her one but none of them had stuck. Francesca she started out and Francesca she stayed. Even the customers who appeared in the darkest hours of the night called her Francesca.

"Francesca?"

"I have to take some time off," she said. "I don't know how long."

"Call when you want to come back," Neo said, unsurprised. He worked with some of the oddest people Francesca had ever met; nothing she could do would ever surprise him.

She called her landlord, told him she'd be away for a while. Francesca considered whether she cared about anything she was leaving behind, and came up with three things: her books, her grandmother's blanket and her grandfather's candy tins. If she was still here when her rent ran out, she'd ask Susannah and C.J. to pick them up and store them for her. The next tenant could have everything else.

She dialed the number most familiar to her and waited for Susannah's voice on the answering machine to stop speaking.

"Susannah? C.J.? I'm going to be out of town for a while."

Francesca wasn't sure what to say next. She should have practiced this message before she started.

"I'm helping out some new friends. He's had a heart attack and they need someone to help them run their coffee shop for a little while. I'll call you, as always, next Sunday."

She didn't know what else to say. Anything more, anything about the House, and Susannah would panic and C.J. would worry. They were on their twenty-five-year delayed honeymoon and she would do nothing to ruin it.

She would have to call them and leave a message every Sunday, otherwise, she wouldn't put it past them to fly home early or to send the police to find her.

She added that to her list along with:

Get clothes, etc. from apartment. If possible.

Check with Marta about Bains Candies.

Should she open the shop?

Should she put a sign on the door about Joshua?

Should she make pastries for breakfasts?

Francesca had only been in the place a couple of days. She had no idea of hours, menu, prices. And she didn't know how to make pastries.

She ran downstairs and turned every one of the lights back on. She began rummaging through the drawers and cupboards behind the counter looking for a menu, a cookbook, an answer, banging them open and shut to keep the fear away. She didn't feel safe here, not at night and not by herself, not the way she did in her room upstairs.

Francesca had snuggled into that room as if she had lived there all her life. She had no clothes, no personal possessions, and she didn't care at all. She felt at home and safe, a combination that astonished her as much as it delighted her. But that feeling only worked in her room. So far. She hoped once Joshua and Marta were back and she didn't feel so much like an intruder that she'd begin to feel that way in the rest of the house.

She was on her knees behind the glass counters when she heard a noise at the front door. She made herself as small as possible.

She peeked around the chocolates on the bottom shelf of the glass case but saw nothing, not even a shadow at the door, but she heard another sound, as if someone was trying to unlock the door.

Screech, screech, screech. The door handle turned, back and forth.

Francesca foolishly thought of her list and made a notation in her mind: *Remember to oil the door handles*.

Someone was trying to open the door.

It had to be Marta coming home. She peered again through the chocolates. This time she saw a shadow bending low over the door handle.

"Not Marta."

She started shivering, wrapping her arms around her shoulders for warmth.

"Now what? What do I do now?" she whispered, her voice harsh in the bright lights.

"Just a darn minute."

She looked again at the shadow bending over the door handle.

"No one would rob a place with the door locked and every single light on."

It wasn't a burglar. Francesca felt slightly better. Maybe it was the cleaner? She added another couple of notations to her mental list and hoped that she'd remember to put them in writing when she got back upstairs.

Check with Marta about suppliers and services.

Cleaners.

Plumbers, electricians, etc.

Do they have a separate number for the shop and the upstairs?

What are the phone numbers?

What about bills?

The list was getting longer and longer and Francesca was still crouched behind the counter, convincing herself she wasn't scared, that she was shaking in her boots because her blood sugar was low. Shaking in her bare feet really; she didn't have boots with her, only sneakers, crusted with blood.

"Just do it," she said, right out loud, no longer caring whether the person at the front door heard her. "Get up."

Her legs continued to shake but she started to

pull herself up, clinging to the countertop. The minute her head topped the glass shelf, the noises at the front door stopped.

"Who are you?" she yelled from behind the counter. "I've called the police," she lied.

"So have I," said a low voice from the front door. "They should be here any minute."

Now Francesca was mad, and that was the only emotion that ever counteracted her fear. She finished hauling herself to her feet and scurried around the counter, grabbing a chair as she did so. She'd seen enough movies to know what to do with it.

She slammed the back of the chair up under the doorknob and stood back, her arms crossed.

"Who are you?" she demanded. "And what are you doing here?"

"I could ask the same of you," said the shadow.

Francesca could only see his outline with all the lights at her back. She stepped back. He, she realized with a thrill of fear, could probably see her much more clearly than she could see him. She slapped at the light switch and turned it off.

She backed away until she felt the cool glass of the counter against her back. She wasn't going to say another word until the cops arrived. He couldn't get in.

Back door. Of course. She grabbed another chair and carried it into the kitchen, wedging it tightly under the doorknob.

Thank God she'd checked all the windows and doors before she'd gone upstairs. Unless he was willing to break a window—and he hadn't done so yet—she was safe until the cops arrived.

But she wasn't convinced he had actually called the police. She looked around the shop for a phone. Ah, there it was. Right where it should be, on the counter right next to a pile of empty gold boxes.

She picked it up and dialed 9-1-1, hoping the universal number worked in this place, hoping there were police.

"We've already had a call from that address," said the professional voice on the other end of the phone line. "A patrol car is on its way.

"Stay on the phone," she said, "until they get there."

Francesca slid down to sit on the floor with her back against the counter, the phone grasped in her hand. She tried not to think about how complicated the conversation with the police was going to be.

She didn't even know what hospital Joshua was in. She didn't know... She didn't even know if he was still alive. Tears slipped from beneath her lashes.

She took another peek around the chocolate boxes. The shadow had disappeared. She couldn't see the kitchen from her spot on the floor, but she listened for any noise from the back.

The doorknob jiggled, a light scratching she could barely hear, and then that noise stopped and, a few moments later, the shadow reappeared at the front door.

Francesca shrank closer to the floor and waited, the phone clutched in her hand and the voice on the other end telling her to remain calm.

She couldn't *remain* calm when she'd hardly ever been calm. She could, though, pretend.

"They're just around the corner," the voice said, "you should hear the sirens now."

Francesca forced her awareness away from the phone and listened.

"I hear them."

"Okay, now just stay on the phone with me. The officers will be with you in a minute."

Francesca waited some more. And she worried. She wasn't sure whether the police would arrest the intruder or her.

All she had to prove her right to be in Mystic Hearts was the ring of three keys Marta had left with her.

CHAPTER 18

Paul Trevor stood on the steps outside Bains Candies, angry and scared. He wasn't sure which emotion was winning, but he knew that combination was deadly.

He'd spent ten years living a life where this particular combination of feelings was a very bad idea. Once that time was over, he'd carefully insulated himself from situations where anger might begin to rule his brain and where fear could overwhelm him.

Yet, ten years on, here they were again.

He'd refused to re-up because of his distrust of those emotions. He'd created a life where he was in control, complete control, of all the circumstances around him.

Except his clients of course.

He grimaced. His clients could send anyone into a towering rage, sometimes with a single look or word. But he wasn't scared of them, even when they got violent. And he loved his job with the kind of passion most men reserved for women.

His clients were mostly sick. If any of them ever hurt him—and they had—it was an accident. None of them were strong enough to hurt a flea on purpose.

All right, a flea maybe, but they didn't care about fleas so if they killed them, again, it was an accident, scratching away in the night.

Paul had seen plenty of evidence of that cleaning up the dorm in the mornings. He spent most mornings with his nose clogged up with the tart aroma of industrial-strength disinfectant, and then his afternoons with the rank odor of men and women who went months without a shower.

But he didn't mind those smells. They meant he was helping people who could no longer help themselves. And Paul had come back from Afghanistan determined to do just that.

He snorted at that thought.

"You came home wanting to drown the memories of those years. You didn't have a single thought in your mind except taking your savings and drinking until you couldn't remember a thing."

Paul tried hard not to remember those first few months as a civilian.

He turned his thoughts away from the past and back to Joshua and Marta.

Where in the hell were they?

Every light in the damn house was on and they didn't answer the door. Someone, someone too spry to be either of them, had been moving around in the shop when he'd gotten here. That person had disappeared but some of the lights were still on.

Paul checked the front and the back doors but couldn't open either of them. He'd often asked Joshua for an extra set of keys. "Just in case," he'd said, but Joshua had only laughed.

"We're fine, Paul, you don't need to worry about us. We may look old but we're in pretty good shape. If you think something's wrong, you have my permission to break in."

And Paul had had to be satisfied with that.

He hadn't felt right about breaking in, though he had tried to pick the front-door lock. When it hadn't worked like it did in the movies, he'd left it.

He tried to be sensible, he really did, and he tried not to think of Joshua and Marta lying dead in a pool of blood in the kitchen.

Paul had done the circuit of the house. If Joshua and Marta were lying in a pool of blood, they were doing it on the second floor.

He just didn't think any murderer, or any burglar for that matter, would be walking around the house having turned on every single light. Whoever was inside had heard him, come to the front door to check him out and then vanished.

Well, sort of vanished. Because Paul knew exactly where the person was, crouching down behind the glass counter. He occasionally caught a glimpse of movement but he hadn't been able to identify the person other than to say with certainty that it wasn't either Joshua or Marta.

He'd called the cops and they were on their way.

"Paul?" the dispatcher had asked. "What are you doing there?"

"Friends of mine own the shop," he'd said, "and something weird's going on."

"Hang in there, bud, I'll send a car over right away."

So Paul was cooling his heels on the front porch while a stranger moved around in his best friends' house. He was not impressed, but he knew better than to do anything stupid.

He needed the cooperation of the police at his place on a daily basis, so he wasn't going to do anything to jeopardize that relationship. Besides, he thought, he'd already figured out that Joshua and Marta were okay, hadn't he?

But if they weren't, and Paul felt the old dragon of fear and anger rearing its ugly head, that stranger was going to be in serious trouble.

The patrol car pulled up to the curb and two cops

got out, one male, one female. Paul didn't know either of them but they seemed to know him, or at least of him.

"Paul? Paul Trevor? I'm Officer Lahr and this is Officer Barker. What's up?"

They were so young, Paul thought, and looking at them made him feel old, so much older than he really was. He had just turned forty-five last year but he felt ancient looking at the fresh-faced cops in front of him.

"My friends Joshua and Marta live here and run this candy store. They don't go anywhere, not at night, anyway, but when I dropped by just now, there was someone in the shop."

"Not your friends?"

"No, this person was young. Joshua and Marta, well, they move differently."

Paul couldn't bring himself to call them old. He never thought of them that way, never had, until he'd seen someone else in their shop and realized why it was he knew it wasn't his friends.

"Were they expecting any visitors?"

"I don't think so. I don't think either of them have any family. And this person—" he glanced back over his shoulder and saw the shadow moving behind the counter "—hid behind the counter when he saw me at the door."

"Let's take a look, okay, Paul." That was such a typical cop thing to do that Paul almost laughed out loud, using his first name to get his cooperation. "You wanna wait down there on the sidewalk?"

It wasn't really a question and Paul took it as it was meant, moving down to the sidewalk, but watching from there to see what would happen.

"Ma'am?"

That surprised Paul. How did they know it was a woman? Could they see her? He still couldn't see anything except faint movement behind the counter until the cops moved in front of the door and blocked his view.

"Ma'am? I'm Officer Lahr and this is Officer Barker," the female officer repeated the words she'd used with Paul. "Can you open the door for us, please?"

Francesca had heard the siren and seen the flashing lights but she hadn't moved until the police called to her from the front door. She told the dispatcher that the police were at the door and hung up the telephone.

She pulled the chair back from under the knob and tried to open the door. It wouldn't. She twisted the knob and jiggled the door in the frame. Still nothing.

Francesca thought of the keys upstairs on the table beside her bed and remembered that she'd had to use the key to lock the old-fashioned front door.

"Hang on," she yelled through the door. "I have the keys upstairs. I'll run and get them."

Once the door was opened and the police had stepped inside, Francesca started.

"That man—" she pointed to the man on the sidewalk "—that man tried to break into the shop. Check the door handle, there are probably marks on it."

"Ma'am." The female police officer stopped Francesca with a hand. "Who are you?"

"Oh, sorry, I'm Francesca Bond. Joshua had a heart attack and Marta's at the hospital with him. She wanted me to stay until she got back."

"Do you have some identification?"

"Upstairs, my wallet's upstairs."

"I'll come with you and you can get it, okay?"

Francesca bristled at the tone of the woman's voice but said nothing. It was going to be hard enough to explain what she was doing at Bains Candies without starting out by antagonizing the police.

Her identification was scanned and taken away by the second cop, the silent one, to the car, presumably to check if she had any outstanding warrants.

"I don't, you know."

"Don't what?"

"Have a police record. Just wait until Marta gets home and she'll tell you that I'm supposed to be here."

Francesca crossed her fingers and hoped that the cop wouldn't ask just when Marta was supposed to be home because Francesca had absolutely no idea, except that she knew Marta wouldn't leave Joshua alone in the hospital.

She turned to the policewoman.

"What's the nearest hospital? I'll phone them."

"You can phone them in a minute."

The silent cop returned and shook his head at the female one.

"Okay, Ms. Bond. Let me tell you what happened. That man outside, Paul Trevor, says he's a friend of the couple who live here. He says he came over to visit and saw someone skulking around."

"I didn't skulk," Francesca insisted. "Someone tried to break in and I was scared so I hid behind the counter. I definitely didn't skulk."

"Okay, you didn't skulk. But Mr. Trevor was suspicious because he couldn't get you to answer the door."

"Yeah, I didn't answer the door because he was trying to break in. He tried the back door, too. Why don't you go see if there are marks on that door?"

Francesca's determination to stay calm and not antagonize the police was not going well.

"*He* tried to break in. I'm the innocent one, I'm supposed to be here. And how do you know he's a friend of Joshua's? I'm the one with the keys. Marta gave *me* the keys, not him.

"Let me call the hospital and talk to Marta. She can straighten this all out. I don't like the idea of that man being out there on the sidewalk.

"You have to take him with you when you go. He should be in jail, shouldn't he? I mean, he tried to break in. Isn't that attempted robbery or something?"

"Ms. Bond—" the woman could barely restrain her amusement "—Ms. Bond, that man really is Paul Trevor. Our dispatcher knows him."

"Don't you find that suspicious? Your dispatcher knows him? How does she know him?"

"Mr. Trevor runs a mission down on the east side. He's an upstanding citizen who's never been in any trouble with the police. If he says he's a friend of Mr. Bains, you can bet he is a friend of Mr. Bains."

"So why was he trying to break in?"

Francesca couldn't believe that the police believed Paul Trevor instead of her.

"I have the keys."

It was her only defense.

And it didn't do her much good. The police kept her there, the man still standing on the sidewalk outside, until she reached Marta on the phone.

"Francesca? What's going on?"

The female cop took the phone from Francesca and spoke.

"Mrs. Bains?"

"Her name isn't Bains," the man from the sidewalk interrupted from the doorway. "She and Joshua aren't married. Her name is Marta Van Iperen. She used to be an opera singer, before..."

Francesca looked at him and realized that he didn't want to think about Marta's throat, didn't want to mention it.

"She was in an accident," Francesca said. "She lost her ability to sing."

"Yeah, that's right." He looked at Francesca and nodded a thank you. "Anyway, her name is Marta Van Iperen."

"Ms. Bond and Mr. Trevor," the cop continued, nodding toward Paul, "called us. *He* says she's an intruder and *she* says he's a burglar."

Paul's face was pale and worried, and Francesca suddenly realized that he wasn't a burglar, that he really was a friend of Joshua and Marta's.

"Where are they?" he asked.

"They're at St. Jude's. Joshua had a heart attack."

The police had finally given her the name of the nearest hospital and she'd called.

Francesca couldn't figure out a way to say those words that wouldn't be painful.

The color returned to Paul's face and he looked slightly less worried. He looked at the cop on the phone.

"So what's *she*—" he pointed at Francesca "—doing here? Why didn't they call me?"

He asked these questions as if the cop were the one in charge and that infuriated Francesca.

"I'm here because Joshua and Marta want me to help them in the shop. Marta gave me the keys to the shop and gave me a room upstairs to stay in.

"I've packed some stuff—" she pointed at the old-fashioned suitcase at the door "—for Marta and Joshua. Does that satisfy you?" Francesca glared at Paul Trevor.

He was the most aggravating man she'd ever met. First he scared her to death by trying to break into the shop, then he accused her of being a thief. What a creep.

She mentally added to her rapidly expanding list:

Check with Marta about Paul Trevor.

She glared over at Paul again.

"Is everything okay, now?" she asked the police.

"It's late—" she glanced at her watch "—ohmiGod, it really is late. I have a lot to do tomorrow. I need to get some sleep."

"Mr. Trevor?" the female police officer asked.

He nodded at her and then nodded once at Francesca. "I guess it's okay."

Francesca slept like the dead when she had once again turned off all the lights, checked all the windows and doors and made her way back upstairs to her room. She didn't even have enough energy to read a single page of *The Keeper of the Bees* though she placed it on the pillow next to her just in case.

She decided the next morning, while in the tiny shower hidden in an alcove in her bathroom next to the tub, to close Bains Candies for a day while she worked out a plan. She carefully handwrote a sign—changing it several times until it was exactly right:

Bains Candies Is Closed Today.
We Will Reopen Tomorrow
At Our Usual Time.

CHAPTER 19

Francesca picked a bouquet of flowers—peonies and lilies and lilacs from the bush at the very back of the huge garden, Peace roses from the bushes at the front door—wrapped them in damp paper towels and plastic bags, and headed for St. Jude's, ignoring the fact that half of the flowers she had in her hands were out of season.

She found Marta in the waiting room on the second floor, Paul Trevor sitting next to her. Francesca turned around and then forced herself to turn back into the waiting room.

"Marta," she said, handing her the flowers, "I've brought these for Joshua. How is he?"

Francesca hadn't really needed to ask, she could tell by the smile on Marta's face that Joshua was going to be okay, but she did want to know how many of the questions on the list that had grown exponentially over the night she could ask.

Marta jumped to her feet and pulled Francesca

into a hug so tight that she thought her ribs might break. But she didn't pull away. Being hugged was something that didn't happen to her very often and Francesca was going to enjoy every minute of it.

"Francesca," Marta said and, because she was so close, Francesca could hear the lovely tones of her voice for the very first time. "He's going to be fine. The doctors think if he eats better, gets a little exercise, takes aspirin every day, he'll be fine. He has to start taking it easy, though, the doctor said. He's too old to be working at the store full-time."

"Oh, Marta, I'm so happy. Can I see him?"

"Not right now, the doctor's in there with him, but he said he'd only be half an hour or so. Come and sit down."

Marta pushed Francesca into the chair next to Paul Trevor and sat down on the other side of her.

"Paul, this is our friend, Francesca Bond. She's going to be helping us in the store from now on."

Paul looked at Francesca and shook his head. "I know the police told her about last night, but I think she's forgotten," he mouthed.

"I haven't forgotten anything. But it's over and you're going to be friends."

Marta used a look that could only be called the death glare on both of them.

"You're *going* to be friends."

And she turned to Francesca as if nothing had happened between them.

"Paul owns and runs a soup kitchen."

"Marta, Marta, Marta. It's not a soup kitchen. It's a restaurant, a good one, too. Just because my customers don't always pay doesn't mean that it's a soup kitchen. I hardly ever serve soup."

"Paul, you always serve soup."

Marta laughed at the man sitting next to Francesca and it was obvious how much she liked him. *You really have to like a person to tease them*, Francesca thought.

The only people she knew well enough and liked enough to tease were Susannah and C.J. That was an aspect of her life she definitely needed to work on.

She started another list, writing it on the pad she carried around in her mind until she got home to Mystic Hearts and was able to write it down on paper.

Make more friends.

Have more fun.

Those two goals weren't going to be easy for Francesca and she wasn't at all sure how to go about accomplishing them. But she thought that right here in St. Jude's was a good start. Because she was pretty sure she had two more friends than she'd had last week.

Joshua and Marta were her friends. And, if Marta had her way, Paul would be a friend as well.

They'd better be; three of them were all going to be living in the same house. Francesca put that scary thought aside and concentrated on what Paul was saying to Marta.

"Okay, okay, I always serve soup. What can I say? I'm a soup kind of guy. But it's damn good soup, if I have to say so myself."

Marta giggled.

"You don't have to say so yourself, I'll say it for you. Paul makes damn good soup. Joshua buys it in bulk for Bains and keeps it in the freezer downstairs."

"What kind of soup?" Francesca didn't know what else to say. She was still stricken by the idea of this particular man running a soup kitchen—oops, a restaurant.

He was big, very big, and strong with it. He was probably a couple of inches shorter than C.J. but whereas C.J. was all lean muscle, Paul was solid. He had to be a weight lifter.

"He's not."

Marta, reading her mind again, answered a question Francesca never would have asked.

"Oh," she said, and waited for Marta to explain.

"He spends his days carrying sacks of potatoes,

stirring gallon pots full of soup, hefting sides of beef and dozens of chickens. Tell her, Paul," Marta said, hiding a cough behind her hands and waving at him to continue.

Francesca wondered how it was that everyone knew exactly what it was that Marta wanted. She supposed it was because they knew her so well, and she hoped that one day she'd be the one Marta asked to continue her story.

"My job is forty percent hard physical labor, thirty percent creative accounting, and thirty percent psychological counseling. The forty percent accounts for these," he pointed at his arms.

Francesca smiled.

"What does the other sixty percent count for?"

"Hmmm, let me see. Okay, creative accounting. I have a little money of my own, I make a little by selling soup to other restaurants, and I get a few grants from various charities and the government. In order to turn that into enough money to run the restaurant and the hotel..."

"The hotel?"

"Oh, yeah, I have twenty beds upstairs for people who need them. Some of them have been there for years, and they pay what they can, usually not very much, the others are for transients who can't get into any other shelter."

A sad expression crossed Paul's face. Marta reached out and touched his arm.

"Go on," Francesca said, to distract him, to ease the sadness in his eyes.

"In order to turn that into enough money, I do a lot of bartering, I don't have any paid employees, and I make absolutely no money."

"What about the other thirty percent?"

"That's the tricky part," he said, his words slowing.

Francesca watched the emotions pass over his face. She'd never met a man with such an expressive face. She could see almost everything he was thinking as soon as he thought it.

Right now, he was feeling in turn joy, disappointment, sadness and a tiny amount of fear. But the fear wasn't for himself, it was for his clients, his friends. It was easy for Francesca to recognize the fear, it was her face's best known expression. The other expressions, on Paul's face, were equally easy to see.

He seemed to have no filters, no necessity to hide anything from the world.

"The other thirty percent? I spend that time helping people get medical assistance, getting them into detox, helping them with their scum landlords or cashing their checks or finding their long-lost families.

"It's hard to cash a check unless you have a bank account and you can't get a bank account unless you have a permanent address. And it's hard to reunite with your family if you don't have a phone or access to a computer for the search."

Francesca saw that Paul had more to say but he wasn't quite ready to say it. She turned to Marta.

"I have a list of questions for you and Joshua. I don't know what to do first," she said. "Will you come home tonight?"

Marta shook her head.

"Close the shop," she said. "We take a vacation around this time every year. Just say we'll be away for a week."

"Are you sure?"

"Joshua will be home by then. He'll help you with the shop, with the menus, and everything else. It can all wait until he's home. It's not that important."

Paul reached over Francesca and grabbed Marta, pulling her into his arms.

"Don't cry, honey, don't cry. Joshua's going to be fine. He's a strong man."

"I can't live without him, Paul."

Marta's ravaged voice reverberated into Francesca's ears, her head right next to Marta's throat.

"I know, Marta," Paul said, his deep voice

sending waves of warmth through Francesca, "I don't know if I can live without him either. But we aren't going to have to. The doctor already said he was going to be okay."

"But what if he's not?"

Francesca wiggled her way out from between Paul and Marta and placed her two hands on top of Marta's shoulders.

"He's going to be fine. I know it," she said and, oddly enough, she really did know it.

Francesca's certainty somehow communicated itself to Marta and all three of them sat back in their chairs, content now to wait for the doctor.

"I spend a big piece of time," Paul continued as if nothing had interrupted him, "just making sure everybody's all right. I listen, mostly, but sometimes, somehow, I know how to say exactly the right thing."

He smiled at Francesca over Marta's head. She wanted to tell him that she hadn't tried to say the right thing, she'd said the true thing.

"And sometimes," he went on, "all they need is for someone to listen to them, someone who doesn't want anything from them, someone who has no agenda. I'm no psychologist, but if there's one thing I've learned over the past ten years, it's that everyone needs someone to listen to them.

"And everyone needs someone who doesn't

judge them. Because not a single one of us hasn't made a mistake in our life, done something we wish we could take back."

Francesca wondered what thing Paul wanted to take back. She knew what Marta's was; she could think of dozens of things she wished she'd never done. But Paul? He seemed so together.

The nurse waved Marta over to the desk.

Marta smiled and left, moving so fast that Francesca was left staring at a blank space where Marta had once been.

"Joshua's room is that way?" she asked and blinked again to make sure she wasn't imagining Marta's disappearance.

"Yep." Paul laughed. "That woman sure can move when she wants to. Let's give them a few minutes and then we can go and see him."

Francesca had a dozen questions she wanted to ask Paul but most of them seemed too personal. She settled for one of the easy ones.

"What's your restaurant called?"

"You won't believe this, but it doesn't really have a name. Well, it does, sort of. But I didn't have any money leftover for a sign, so I looked around the junkyards and picked up an old neon sign from a café that closed down twenty-five years ago.

"I have a friend who works in neon and he

helped me fix it up. The sign says Good Food, so that's what my place is called."

Every town and every city had a restaurant with a Good Food sign outside. And, as if it were a curse on the signs themselves, almost every one of them managed to lose the final letters of the words, leaving a sign saying Goo Foo. Francesca had been to a few of those restaurants over the years; she'd even worked in one in a small town in the south.

She had a fondness for those words.

"Do all the letters work?"

"They do now. When I bought the sign, a couple of the letters were missing, but Jess fixed them up and the sign's perfect. Bright red neon and it shines like hope in that neighborhood."

Paul's face shone as he spoke of the sign.

Francesca was certain that those two simple words were somehow a symbol of what he was trying to do, of his dream. She envied him that symbol. But her dream was internal and she didn't think there was a way that she could turn it outside herself. Fear didn't work that way.

For her, fear was a turning inward, a search for control. But listening to Paul talk about his sign, she wondered if she'd been trying to deal with her fear in the wrong way. Maybe what she needed was a symbol, a way to externalize the fear, set it outside of herself.

Francesca put that thought aside to think about when she had more time. And more sleep. Enough things had changed in her life; she had no energy for anything further.

Thanks to Paul Trevor, she'd had too little sleep last night, as well.

Francesca sighed and leaned against the chair back, her T-shirt sticking to the fluorescent-blue plastic. This hospital needed air-conditioning. She fanned herself with the list she'd brought with her.

"This hospital needs more than air-conditioning," Paul said. "I think it needs a complete overhaul. Or maybe they should just tear it down and start again."

"The property's probably worth too much. They'll never find as good a location."

"Maybe not, but one-hundred-year-old bricks aren't too sanitary. Have you looked out the window?"

Francesca shook her head.

"Well, I did. And the bricks aren't red, they're black with grime. And they're flaking away. A strong wind might blow this place down. And even a tiny earthquake might knock it over."

"Thanks, that makes me feel much better. As if I didn't have enough to worry about without thinking about this building blowing down or collapsing around me."

Paul laughed.

"We haven't had an earthquake in this part of the country. Not ever."

Francesca gave herself a little shake and concentrated on the combined aromas of the flowers she still held in her hands.

"You're not from here, are you?" Paul asked.

"Why?"

She wasn't in the mood to answer any questions. She had too many to ask.

"Because most people from around here are scared of tornadoes, not earthquakes. If you're scared of earthquakes, you must be from the West Coast somewhere."

Francesca cursed. She hated it when she gave herself away. One of the ways she blended into the landscape was always, always, always, to look as if she belonged wherever she was. She had a great gift for mimicry, so accents weren't a problem, but when she was tired or stressed, she tended to forget small things like tornadoes versus earthquakes.

"I've been to the West Coast," she compromised.

Paul jumped to his feet when Marta came back. "Can we go in now?"

She nodded and tugged Francesca to her feet.

"He wants to see me?"

Francesca realized that she, too, was beginning

to understand Marta's facial expressions. She suspected that Paul and Joshua did it to save Marta from having to speak, but Francesca had done it because she saw the sentence in her mind.

It had looked like dialogue in a novel. Indent. Quotation marks. Sentence. Period. End quotation marks. New paragraph.

Marta's beautiful mouth widened and her slightly crooked teeth appeared. It wasn't a smile, not exactly; instead it was an acknowledgment of a shared moment, a growing together.

Francesca squeezed Marta's hand to show that she understood and then followed her into Joshua's room.

Paul followed too closely behind. She felt his breath and it raised the hairs on the back of her neck. But it wasn't fear she felt, it was something else, something she hadn't felt since she was a teenager.

Paul's breath on her neck gave her goose bumps, goose bumps that traveled up and down her spine, pooling somewhere around its base, warm and sweet and more frightening than the darkest, emptiest alley.

CHAPTER 20

Joshua had waited impatiently for Francesca. He needed to talk to her and explain about the magic of Mystic Hearts.

He also had to tell her about the many things to be done at the candy store. But knowing about Mystic Hearts was far more important than anything he needed to say about making candies or buying supplies.

Marta suggested that he hold off telling her about Mystic Hearts, reminding him that the next Midsummer eve was still almost a year away.

"But what if something happens to me?" he said.

"Don't say that."

"I need to tell her," Joshua insisted.

Marta shrugged her shoulders and turned away to hide the tears Joshua knew she was shedding. Neither of them could bear the thought of being parted.

"Marta. You know it's important. I'm going to be

fine, but I don't want to leave her without giving her every piece of information she'll need."

"I'll give her the stories," Marta whispered.

"The stories?"

"I've been writing them down."

"All of them?"

"Every one you've told me."

"Marta." Joshua held out his arms to her. "You're amazing. You're beautiful and you're smart. No man is as lucky as I am."

"You're just happy you don't have to tell those stories again, that's all."

Paul and Francesca sat on one side of Joshua's bed, Marta on the other, holding his hand.

Francesca had steeled herself to see Joshua hooked up to machines, but she hadn't been able to imagine how pale he was. It scared her, the way the color had leached out of his skin, the way his cheeks seemed to have shrunken in on themselves.

"Francesca, you have to stop worrying about me. I'm going to be fine."

Joshua reached out his other hand and touched the back of Francesca's. His hand was chill and damp.

Francesca looked at the floor, trying to stop the tears she felt prickling in her eyes.

"Paul," Joshua continued, "I need to talk to Francesca alone. Can you come back later on this afternoon? I know it's your busiest time, but..."

Paul nodded.

"I'll be back just before dinner, okay? I'll bring the crib board."

The room felt bigger with Paul Trevor out of it. There was more air to breathe, and Francesca took advantage of it, catching up on all the oxygen she'd missed since she'd arrived at St. Jude's and found Paul sitting next to Marta.

"Here's my list," she said, handing the page of questions to Joshua. "But Marta said I should close the shop for a week so none of them are too urgent."

Joshua patted her hand, then Marta's.

"You've done the right thing, Marta. A week and I'll be back in fighting form."

The two women shared a glance. If they had anything to say about it, the glance said, he was going to take more than a week to recuperate.

Anything you need, Marta's eyes said to Francesca, *you ask me and we'll work it out.*

I can handle things at the shop, Francesca replied, *I just need some guidance.*

Joshua needs to feel he's useful, Marta's eyes signaled.

I'll leave the questions for him, shall I? Francesca flashed the list she'd brought with her.

Leave them with me, Marta answered, *I'll write down the answers for you*.

"Joshua, I've gotta go now. I need to figure out where everything is. I'll leave the list with Marta. She can write down your answers."

"Good girl," Joshua said, his voice fading. "Good girl."

"I'll see you tomorrow," Francesca mouthed to Marta over Joshua's nodding head. "Same time?"

Marta nodded and whispered a response.

"He needs sleep more than anything. But if you need any help, call Paul. His number is at the top of the pad next to the phone in the shop."

Francesca nodded, but her nod was a lie. The last person she would call would be Paul Trevor. She'd call her mother in Italy before she'd telephone Paul Trevor, and if her mother had been the last person on earth, Francesca wouldn't have called her. She guessed that meant that even if she and Paul Trevor were the last two people on earth, she wouldn't call him.

But she didn't have a choice.

Paul Trevor was waiting for her at the nurse's station.

"Can I give you a lift home?"

Francesca's heart soared. He called Mystic Hearts her home. Maybe she could stay there for a while, at least until Joshua felt well enough to run the shop again.

"Okay, but only because I have a lot to do when I get there. The garden needs to be watered. And I have to check on what's in the kitchen and decide what to do so none of the food spoils. And I probably need to do something about the chocolates in the case."

He tucked her hand into his arm and led her out of the hospital.

"My truck's in the lot at the back."

The drive home was all of five minutes long; it had taken Francesca almost half an hour to walk over in the morning. But she still didn't want to buy a car.

She liked buses, liked walking, even liked riding her bike. She felt safer that way. Cars made her nervous and she especially hated turning left into a busy intersection.

She rented a car occasionally, mostly when she was moving from one apartment to another, but she hated every minute of it. People just didn't pay attention so no matter how carefully she adhered to the safe driving rules she'd learned in driving school, she still worried about everyone else. *They* didn't seem to have taken the defensive driving course or if they had, they'd forgotten everything they'd learned in it.

The drive back to Mystic Hearts was silent. Francesca was thinking about lunch; she suspected Paul was wondering why Joshua had asked her to take care of the shop instead of him.

"I'm glad Joshua has you to look after the shop," he said, "and I'm really sorry I scared you last night."

Francesca had expected anything but those two statements from Paul Trevor, though when she thought about it, she didn't know why. Except for trying to break into the shop last night, he'd been a perfectly reasonable human being. In fact, he'd been much more than that.

So why was she still expecting him to be a jerk? She shelved that question for later, along with all the other things on her secondary list.

"You did scare me," she replied, "but that was because I've never lived in a house before. I've always been in apartment buildings where there were lots of other people around to call if someone tried to break in."

He laughed so loud and boisterously that it invited Francesca to join in. She giggled for a moment and then went back to the conversation.

"Seriously, though," she said, "are thefts a problem? In my neighborhood..."

He stopped her, touching her arm.

"Where do you live?"

Francesca didn't know how to answer that question. She didn't see how this world could also contain her neighborhood, her life. But it must have something similar if Paul ran a mission—must still contain the sad, lonely people who often slept in her alley.

So she answered as best she could.

"I live in a neighborhood like yours, I think."

"Oh," he said quietly, "I get it now. No wonder you were scared. Some days I'm scared walking those streets."

Francesca looked at Paul and laughed. She laughed until she had tears running down her face. She laughed until she started coughing so hard she couldn't breathe. She laughed until Paul handed her a bottle of water.

"Drink this. Your face is turning blue."

She took a sip. Of course it went down the wrong way. She spit it up all over her shirt and Paul's dashboard. She couldn't possibly embarrass herself any further.

Paul pulled over to the curb and stopped the truck a little too abruptly for Francesca's liking.

"Are you okay?"

He sounded a bit fed up, even though he did reach over and rub her back until she stopped coughing.

Francesca couldn't blame him for being annoyed.

First she laughed at him until she cried and then she spewed water all over his truck. If she never saw him again, she was pretty sure it would be too soon for Paul Trevor.

Now that she knew she wouldn't see him again, she very much wanted to. She liked his face. He'd lived in that face for a very long time, and he'd lived hard. And she liked his body. He was built tough, solid and bulky.

"I'm fine," she insisted, shaking off his solicitude. "Really. But I think I'll walk the rest of the way home."

Francesca felt the heat in her face spread to her chest and her shoulders. She knew her skin was crimson with shame, she'd seen it that way often enough.

She'd never been any good at hiding her emotions though she'd spent a fair amount of money trying. As always with problems, Francesca had tried to solve this one by taking courses: How to Deal with Shyness; Embarrassment 101; You Too Can Be Calm, Cool and Collected. None of them had worked.

Every emotion she experienced blossomed on her skin. She turned devil-red with anger, with joy, with shame and embarrassment. She turned ghoul-white with fear and sorrow. She turned green when she was sick, though she'd never cared enough for anyone to turn green with jealousy.

"You don't have to walk home. It's right on my way and I promised Marta I'd take care of you."

Francesca's quick anger increased the heat under her skin and she knew that instead of red, she was well on her way to turning purple.

"I don't need taking care of."

She flung open the door of the car, tripped on her way out, but managed to save herself before her nose hit the pavement. Two skinned knees were a small price to pay for getting out of Paul Trevor's presence before she did one more incredibly stupid thing.

"Francesca. Don't run. At least let me drive you home," he called after her as she limped down the street.

She ignored him and the red heat burning the back of her neck. She heard him put the truck in Drive and follow along beside her.

"Francesca, come on. What's the problem? I'm sorry if I upset you. Let me drive you home."

She ducked into a narrow alley, the shadows lying so deep at its edges that she had no idea what to expect as she entered it. But she didn't care, anything was better than getting back into that truck. Absolutely anything.

The truck pulled up at the end of the alley and she heard the door open and Paul's voice calling to her.

"Francesca? Are you there?"

She ignored the voice and concentrated ferociously on navigating the rubble lining the alley. She ignored the skittering of the rats in the Dumpsters and the foul odors they stirred up.

"Now what?" she said to herself as she faced a blank wall at the end of the alley. She wished for claws or spider senses or the ability to teleport herself through the wall. None of them appeared.

She pretended to be fascinated by the concrete-block wall. Anything to avoid turning around. She counted the blocks—twenty-seven across and thirty-two high. She analyzed the color, puke-green with just a hint of dirty cream underneath. She tried to decide whether or not to add the senses of touch and smell to her exploration.

Paul touched her shoulder and put his palm over her mouth.

His voice breathed into her ear.

"Don't scream," he said, the whisper hoarse and low.

Francesca nodded vigorously and waited for the palm to leave her face. She was prepared to kick, then scream. She took a deep breath in preparation.

"Don't scream, Francesca."

She swallowed the scream and spoke instead. "Paul?"

CHAPTER 21

Paul Trevor dropped her off at the curb in front of Bains Candies. He hadn't spoken a word to her, nor she to him, since he'd told her not to scream, but Francesca could still hear the murmur of his voice in her ear, still taste the faint menthol flavor of the hospital soap when he'd clapped his palm over her mouth.

Francesca scurried up the steps like a mouse running from a cat, wanting nothing more than to disappear into her own little mouse hole.

She plopped herself down on the nearest chair and tried to relax. The humming of the refrigeration in the glass case and the almost imperceptible buzz of the fluorescent lights began to soothe her, as did the cheerful birds and the sprinklers hissing on the next-door lawns.

One more thing she needed to add to her list—sprinkling. Oh, yeah, and garbage regulations.

This fill-in job was turning out to be far more

complicated than she'd expected. Joshua in the hospital, and Marta with him, had massively increased the complications.

"Hot chocolate," she said, "I need a cup of hot chocolate. With Grand Marnier."

It didn't matter to Francesca that the day was as warm as an oven, or that she never drank in the middle of the day. Today she needed a pick-me-up before she started writing down the mental list she'd been composing all day.

She dashed into the kitchen and opened every one of the cupboards. She took a quick inventory, but knew she'd never remember where to find the vanilla or whether the coffee cups were in the cupboard beside or above the sink.

She grabbed the milk from the fridge, poured a cupful into a saucepan and turned on the burner. She watched the blue flame heat up the pan. Gas stoves had the same effect on Francesca as the ocean did on some people. That blue flame relaxed her, pulled the tension from her muscles and slowed her heartbeat.

Now she was relaxed, she could forget the sentence that had spooked her.

"I don't remember what he said," she lied to herself. And proceeded to reimagine the ride home.

She didn't get mad. She didn't run. She didn't make a fool of herself. Paul Trevor didn't chase her into the alley and she didn't want to scream when he touched her. Everything was as it had been when she'd gotten in the car, a possible new friend, a slowly blooming relationship.

There, she'd done it, created a much more satisfactory ride home, with a satisfying ending.

Hot chocolate in hand, she went upstairs to her room. The drink and the rocking chair completed her treatment. She knew what she needed to do and was going to do it, whether she liked it or not.

An hour after walking in the door, Francesca was ready to start.

She dialed the number listed on the pad next to the phone.

"Good Food," Paul's voice answered.

"Come on over," she said, "I need some help."

"Need?" Paul repeated.

"Need," Francesca agreed.

"I'll be right there."

"Stop at the liquor store and pick up some Grand Marnier." She paused. "Please."

Francesca hadn't found any alcohol in her search of the kitchen though she knew from her first night at Mystic Hearts there had to be some in the house. Just another thing she didn't know.

Grand Marnier was Francesca's favorite drink.

Susannah and Francesca had a history together

of drinking Grand Marnier. The first time the two of them had got drunk was drinking Polar Bears—hot chocolate and Grand Marnier—and watching the New Year's Day swim.

They laughed their fool heads off at the old guys galumphing into the ocean, turning around and screeching right back out again. They giggled when the buff lifeguards pulled off their sweats and dove into the freezing water, slicing through it like dolphins in an IMAX film.

They shivered watching the gray waves roll up on the beach, propelled by a chilly wind blowing off the waves. That's when they decided on the hot chocolate and Grand Marnier.

It was the first New Year's after Francesca had moved out and they headed back to her tiny room, shaking from the cold, their feet frozen solid.

Susannah had seen Polar Bears in a movie or something and it seemed so sophisticated to them. Susannah, already passing for twenty-one, walked into a liquor store and bought the Grand Marnier, while Francesca stopped at the corner store for hot chocolate and milk.

It didn't really count as drinking, they decided later—days later, actually, when their eyes and heads and stomachs had stopped rebelling. It hadn't counted because it hadn't tasted like alcohol.

Grand Marnier was their comfort drink of choice, although Francesca had never since drank enough of it to give her a hangover as severe as the first one. *Today*, she thought, *today might be the day to break her record*.

She hurried back downstairs and waited for Paul; her fingernails tapping on the glass counter, counting and recounting the divinity bars.

Paul and Marta arrived at the door at the same moment. They hammered on the glass. Francesca had forgotten to unlock it.

"Marta?"

Francesca had expected Paul, but hadn't expected Marta, who shouldn't have to knock to get into her own house nor should Francesca be inviting her in. Francesca's face turned beet-red.

"Marta, I'm so sorry. I forgot I had the only keys. Come on in."

"Paul called me," Marta whispered. "He thought maybe I could help and Joshua's sleeping."

Francesca wondered if she'd have an emotion burn on her face by the end of the day; it had never happened before but today was a day in a million.

Francesca must have said at least part of that sentence out loud because Paul repeated her words.

"An emotion burn?"

"The emotional equivalent of a sunburn. If your

face turns red more than once a day, maybe the blood vessels expand or pop or something and you end up with a burn. Just like a sunburn only you get it from emotions."

Marta and Paul shared the same look. Francesca had no trouble recognizing it—it was the one that said, *Are you an idiot?* They didn't say anything, but then they didn't have to.

"Look, I've spent the whole day wallowing in emotions. I've cried more today than I have in ten years. I've been embarrassed so many times that I can't count them. I've been scared and I've been enraged. Just sit down and shut up."

She guided them to the table closest to the kitchen and brought out three empty cups.

"Give," she ordered Paul, who pulled an unopened bottle of Grand Marnier from a bag and handed it over without question.

"Do you want something other than Grand Marnier?" she asked Paul.

"Water, please."

Francesca pointed to the kitchen. Paul laughed.

"I'm the guest, you go."

"No, you go. I'm busy."

She opened the bottle and held it over Marta's empty cup, who nodded yes. Francesca poured them each a cup of Grand Marnier.

Paul returned from the kitchen with a glass and a pitcher of water.

"Now talk," he demanded. "What's up?"

"I'm going to be staying here and helping Joshua and Marta while Joshua's under the weather."

Paul and Marta nodded.

"And?" Paul added.

Francesca had carefully considered that final phrase as soon as she'd seen Marta on the stoop. She didn't want to say *sick;* that implied a cold or the flu or something. She didn't want to say *in the hospital;* she expected to stay for at least a little while after he got home. She didn't want to say anything at all that might imply he wasn't coming home. And soon.

Marta had looked frightened enough without any help from ill-considered words.

Marta said, as if she'd read Francesca's worry, "We hope she'll stay longer."

Francesca would stay as long as she was needed; after that, staying would constitute charity on their part and a declaration of need on hers. Francesca was trying to get over her inability to accept help; she wasn't over it yet.

She smiled at Marta.

"So I need some help."

Each time Francesca said those words, it got

easier. Maybe asking for help wasn't such a bad thing. Maybe, she thought, maybe friends and family really wanted to help, even enjoyed helping. Francesca put that thought away but promised herself to come back to it some other time.

"I can't do this on my own," she said again, "I need help."

"What can I do?" Paul asked.

"I have a week to learn to make pastries and candy. I'm not a bad cook," she added. "I make the best prime rib and garlic mashed potatoes you'll ever eat."

Francesca pondered that sentence, and then, for the first time, told the truth about her cooking.

"I learned to cook prime rib because it was the most expensive thing I could think of and my friends Susannah and C.J. were always taking me out for meals. I wanted to repay them. I wanted to be extravagant."

Marta leaned over the table and wrapped her arms around Francesca so tightly that she had to wiggle out from them.

"You're going to strangle me," she complained, the words belying the brilliant smile on her face.

Francesca had watched Joshua and Marta. And she envied that physical warmth Marta had just shown her, that ability to reach out and with a single light touch of your hand, convey so much. Love. Comfort. Humor.

For the first time in her life, Francesca began to see what she was missing. Independence was one thing, solitude another.

But first she had to deal with the cooking problem.

"I can cook meals," she said. "Meat, potatoes, casseroles. I'm a whiz with pasta. But I can't bake a thing.

"Bread. I can't bake bread. I burn it. Or it's burned on the outside and raw on the inside. Or it comes out looking like a pancake instead of a loaf of bread. I need to make muffins and scones. I need to learn to make things for Bains Candies."

She grinned crookedly at Paul.

"I hear you're a great pastry chef. Teach me to bake. Please."

She turned to Marta. "I took a quick look but I didn't find a menu. Where is it?"

Marta opened the big black bag at her side and pulled out Francesca's list. She handed it over with a smile. Each of the items had been answered in spidery black handwriting.

"Joshua dictated the answers, I wrote them down."

Under *Menu?*, Marta had written: *There isn't one. I just make whatever I feel like and people either eat it or they don't. Mostly they do.*

"That's helpful," Francesca said, sarcasm coloring her voice. "So now what do I do?"

"You learn to make the best scones in the city and while you're learning, I help you cook."

Paul smiled at her.

"It's not that hard. Really."

"I have a week. Can you teach me in a week?"

"We'd better get started," Paul said. "I spent years learning how to make pastries. A one-week intensive course will definitely be a challenge."

CHAPTER 22

Paul had left half an hour ago, promising to gather up all the recipe books, utensils and gadgets they'd need for the first lesson. And then he'd return to take Marta back to the hospital.

"Marta?"

Marta jumped, as if she'd been deep in thought about somewhere or something a long way away.

"Hmm?"

"What about the candies? Does Paul know how to make candies? Is there a recipe book?"

"Joshua's great-grandfather made candies. He passed the recipes on to Joshua's grandfather, who passed them on to Joshua's father, who passed them on to Joshua, who still uses those recipes. He's got them memorized. He doesn't need them anymore, he's been doing it for so long."

"Can he write them down?"

Francesca started to panic. If she didn't have the candy recipes, what was she going to do? Bains

Candies was about candies; the pastries and coffee and hot chocolate were just a way to accommodate the neighbors.

She had started with pastries because she knew she could conquer them with Paul's help. Without Joshua's recipes, though, the whole candy thing was going to be a bust.

She'd spent a few days over several years watching her grandfather make candies. She'd even helped him with it, but she'd lost his recipes and she'd never gotten any further than stirring the pot on special occasions. And then only after the heat had been turned off on the stove.

When she'd turned thirty, she had found her grandfather's candy tins when she'd moved from one city to another. She'd looked and looked for the recipes she was sure she'd stored with the tins, but they were lost, along with so much else.

Moving two or three times in a year wasn't at all conducive to holding on to keepsakes. Francesca figured she lost at least one item every move. She had a lot of lost memories.

Francesca tried not to worry too much about the things she lost. She told herself that the fewer things she had, the fewer things to move. She'd pared her life down to a minimum. She owned nothing she couldn't move herself, nothing that wouldn't fit into a rented pickup truck. The bulk of her belongings fit into boxes; the bigger items mostly came apart for easy moving.

But finding the candy tins and losing the recipes had bugged her. So she'd tried to make candy.

She found a book at a secondhand bookstore and had loved the title: *Sweets for the Sweet-Hearted*. She bought it even though that single book had constituted her entire book-buying budget for the month.

She'd spent too much money and too much time trying to get even the simplest recipe in the damn book to work. She'd eaten liquefied fudge, thrown away crystallized caramel, spat out gooey peanut brittle, and spent weeks with the smell of burned sugar worming its way into her dreams.

Worse than all of that, when she'd finally given up and taken the recipe book back to the bookstore, they'd refused to take it back. They'd laughed when they'd opened the book to the page where she'd tried, unsuccessfully, to sponge off the chocolate fudge. Wouldn't even give her a credit for another book. So it sat on her shelf, mocking her every time it caught her eye.

"Paul has the recipes," Marta added.

"Oh."

What she wanted to say was "Oh, no."

Everything was conspiring to make sure Francesca

couldn't walk away from her attraction to Paul Trevor, couldn't change her mind about changing her life.

"I've already asked him to give you a hand with the candy making. He's almost as good as Joshua."

"Thanks, Marta," Francesca quickly replied. "But maybe I'll just get Paul to give me the candy recipes. He's already doing too much for me, helping me learn to make pastries."

Francesca crossed her fingers behind her back. She probably couldn't figure them out. Not by herself, but she was definitely going to try.

"No, no," Marta said. "Joshua wants Paul to give you a hand."

Marta had played her trump card. Francesca couldn't refuse Joshua, not while he was sick. She wouldn't allow herself to even think about the other possibility. He was going to get well enough to come back to Mystic Hearts, and somehow, though she didn't know how, Mystic Hearts would help him get better.

Francesca knew that the house had something, some ability she couldn't define, knew it as clearly as she knew that Mystic Hearts would help her to get better, help her change her life. Already it was having an effect on her.

"Okay," she said, "I'll talk to Paul about it when

he comes by to drop off the recipes and utensils and pick you up."

"No," Marta said.

"No? Why not?"

"Because I've been away from the hospital too long."

"Right. Right. Of course. You have to get back. Let me pack up some of the chocolates for the nurses."

She hadn't had much time to review Joshua's answers to her questions, but he'd been clear about one thing. The chocolates were made without preservatives, they only lasted a few days and Francesca wasn't going to be able to eat them all.

Send them over to Good Food, Marta had written for Joshua. *I usually send over a couple of boxes a week, anyway, so send everything you won't be able to eat.*

Francesca threw chocolates into boxes willy-nilly.

She knew she should be careful, she'd seen chocolatiers package chocolates in the high-end malls. She even knew that she should be using the white cotton gloves from the box beside the case, instead she shoved them in boxes, piling them one on top of the other without regard for their shapes or flavors.

She did the same with another row of chocolates, filling boxes and boxes for Paul Trevor and Good Food.

She kept back a single tray, throwing a handful of each kind she packed onto that tray so she could try them all.

She didn't hear the truck pull up, but she heard the horn just as she finished the tenth box.

"That's it," she said to Marta. "I'll carry these out to the truck for Paul."

She handed two boxes to Marta. "These are for the nurses. They might as well enjoy some of them."

Francesca turned to take her boxes out to the truck. She wasn't sure which emotion was stronger, the desire to see Paul Trevor again or the desire to run away and hide.

But Francesca had figured out one thing last night—she had to keep going forward, moving ahead, carrying on. And that meant she had to see Paul.

He stood leaning against the truck in the sunlight, relaxed and comfortable in a dark T-shirt and faded jeans. He smiled as she came down the stairs, boxes of candy balanced in her hands.

"Let me help you," he said, taking the teetering boxes from the top. "Oops, I guess I'm not supposed to say that, am I?"

Francesca felt her face redden, but she didn't feel the anger that normally accompanied it. She shrugged.

"Thanks, Paul. Look, I'm…"

"Don't worry about it." He took the rest of the boxes and placed them in the truck. "I understand fear," he said, "I've been there."

And this time the haunted look in his eyes convinced her. He did know.

"I can't help it. When I'm scared I get angry, and I run."

He touched his hand to the side of her face, then leaned forward until his lips were only a breath away from hers.

"You don't need to run from me."

Francesca blinked up at him.

"I won't," she said. "I won't run."

Marta held the chocolate boxes, frowning at the weight of them. She hadn't watched while they'd been packed, but she was willing to bet that Francesca had tumbled the perfectly crafted chocolates into the box with no regard for their safety.

She guessed it didn't matter. The nurses would love them anyway, and they wouldn't be wasted.

She waited until Francesca had gone out through the front door and then took the letter from her bag. She placed it in the exact center of the table, underneath dishes and cutlery, picked up the bag and the chocolates and headed for the car.

She'd been away from Joshua for too long. She knew, instinctively, that he was going to be okay this time, but she wasn't sure about the future.

The first attack might have been overwork, bad diet, stress—although Joshua seemed to be the least stressed person she knew—but the second one was a sign. It was a sign they needed to get things settled.

They needed to give up Mystic Hearts. They needed to give it over to Francesca. They needed to eat better, to rest more, to relax and enjoy the rest of their lives.

They needed to get married.

CHAPTER 23

She handed Paul her boxes of chocolates to add to the ones already in the truck. Francesca had already taken the recipes from Paul and turned to go up the stairs into the store, while Paul stood staring after her.

"Paul." Marta poked him to get his attention. "Let's get going. You can worry about Francesca later. I need to get to the hospital. I've got something I need to do."

She sat in the truck while he hurried after Francesca, catching her on the steps.

"I'll be back later to start the lessons."

Francesca shrugged and hurried into the shop, shutting the door behind her, then pulling down the blinds to get away from the piercing gaze of Paul Trevor.

He was a problem for later.

She had two projects for today: begin learning to make pastries and begin learning about Mystic Hearts.

She would use the time before Paul's return to go over Joshua's answers to her list to see whether there was anything she needed to be doing right away.

The dishes on the table needed to be shifted to the next table over. Francesca had begun to think of this particular table as her table. It would have been easier to sit at a clean table, but Francesca didn't even consider that. She just bent over and picked up the cups and plates and cutlery and moved them.

Underneath everything there was a white envelope addressed to her in the same spiky handwriting as on the list.

"Marta? Why would she leave me a letter?"

Francesca panicked.

"Joshua. Something's really wrong with Joshua and she couldn't tell me in person." She paused in her mumbling.

"No, wait, it can't be that. She looked fine. If it was Joshua, I'd have been able to tell."

Instead of opening the letter and dispelling her worries, Francesca paced, the letter in her hand. She'd learned this avoidance technique over the years as a way to deal with unpaid bills and other worries.

Twenty steps across the shop one way, twenty steps back. This was much better pacing than in her tiny apartment, there she took five steps and had to turn around. Pacing at home made her dizzy and she generally gave it up quite quickly. Bains Candies gave her lots of room so she kept going.

Fifteen minutes later, Francesca took a deep breath, came to her senses and sat back down at the table.

"You can't put this off forever," she said, giving herself a pep talk.

She did this often, though it never really worked. It was a way of working herself up to the inevitable. The pep talk didn't make her feel better; it just distracted her mind while her fingers did whatever was necessary.

Francesca couldn't avoid opening the envelope any longer. She pulled a single thin sheet of obviously hospital-issue paper from the envelope. The writing filled the entire front and back of the paper, written in the tiniest of letters. She unfolded the paper and read.

Francesca:

I've given you Joshua's list. It will answer most of your questions. I'm sure that either I or Paul Trevor can answer anything else you need to know about Bains Candies.

What Paul can't answer, and neither can

I, are the questions I know you will have about Mystic Hearts. Bains Candies, while a part of the house, isn't the whole of it.

I know you will have felt Mystic Hearts's presence, it is what brought you back to us yesterday.

It is not my place to tell you the story of Joshua and Mystic Hearts, but Joshua has given me permission to point you in the right direction.

Over the years, Joshua has told me stories of what has happened in the house, of the many people who have been attracted to it and saved by it. I have no answer to the question you must be asking: What the hell are you talking about?

It is a magical place, but that is all I can tell you about that. I have no idea what kind of magic it is, how it manifests itself or what triggers the magic. Joshua and Mystic Hearts saved my life and I have seen it do the same for others.

In a book in our room, I have written down all the stories told to me by Joshua over the years. These stories are not the complete story of Mystic Hearts, some of it you will have to hear from Joshua himself, but the stories will keep you company in the evenings while you are waiting for our return.

In the closet in our bedroom there is a wooden box on the top shelf. Use the chair next to the door to stand on—that's what I do. The box is locked.

I kept this book secret from Joshua until yesterday. That is why the box is locked.

The key is in the top drawer of the dresser to the right of the closet. Go up there now, Francesca, and take the book out of the box. Place it on your bedside table and each night before you fall asleep, read one of the stories.

You do not need to read these stories in the order in which they're written. They were not told to me in the order in which they happened. Dip into these stories, immerse yourself in them. You will be astonished by what you find in this book.

Good luck, my child.

Marta

Francesca wanted to run upstairs and begin reading Marta's stories. She wanted to run out the front door and hurry home, never to return to this house. She wanted to…

"Francesca? What are you doing sitting there?"

"I'm waiting for you. You said you'd be back after you dropped Marta off. What else would I be doing?"

Paul reached for the paper still resting in Francesca's fingers.

"What's this? A love letter?"

"No, not a love letter. But a mystery," Francesca replied. "It's from Marta."

She released her fingers, let Paul take the page from her and waited while he read the letter.

"Shall we go upstairs?" Paul asked. "The pastry lesson can wait."

"Maybe so, but we should put away the supplies before we go book hunting."

She picked up one of the bags Paul had deposited on the floor.

"What's in this? Bricks? It weighs a ton."

Francesca hefted the bag. Glass tinkled.

"This doesn't sound like pastry-making supplies to me. And you don't seem to drink. What did you buy?"

She put the bag on the table and peered in. Jars of tomato sauce, jam, pickles and pickled beets. Artichoke hearts.

"Huh?"

She opened another bag. This one actually did contain bricks. Bricks of ice cream. Chocolate.

Vanilla. Vanilla English toffee. Strawberry Crème. And three kinds of cheese.

The next bag had bake-it-yourself frozen bread and half a dozen pounds of butter. Half salted, half unsalted. Cans of tuna. Smoked oysters.

"You're planning a party?"

"No, but I thought if I was spending the next few days over here, I needed to make sure there was food."

"Okay," Francesca said, "let's get the groceries put away and get the book."

Five minutes later the two of them stood in front of the door at the end of the upstairs hall. Like the door to Francesca's room, it had glass knobs and faded cream paint.

"I don't feel right about this," Francesca said.

"I know. It's kind of like going into your parents' bedroom. You never know what you're going to see."

"It's not that." Francesca groaned. "Not really. It's just that..."

She paused. She wasn't sure why she felt uncomfortable about going into this room. Marta had given her permission, had asked her to enter. But something was stopping her.

"I'm not sure... I guess I'm not sure I want to know that much about this place. I already feel so tied to it. It's the first place I've ever really felt at home. It's going to be hard enough to leave. Maybe the less I know the better."

"Don't tell me you can turn around and go back downstairs without getting the book."

Francesca shrugged, reaching for Paul's shoulder. She needed to hold on to something. With the other hand, she turned the knob and pushed the door until it stood wide open. She still didn't want to cross the threshold.

Paul pulled her through the door. The chair beside the door was an old wooden ladderback, sturdy enough for Francesca to stand on. Paul, still holding Francesca's hand, pulled it over to the closet and opened the door.

"There. Look, there's the box. I'll get it if you want."

"No, I'll get it."

"Get it now, then, because I'm hungry and I hear strawberry ice cream calling me."

The wooden box was lighter than it looked, with its aged oak and tarnished hinges. Francesca handed it to Paul and stepped down from the chair. She carefully closed the closet door, placed the chair back exactly where she'd found it, and ushered Paul out of the room, closing the door behind her.

She breathed a sigh of relief. Being in that room,

with its mingled scents of Marta and Joshua, had made her uncomfortable.

She had tried not to look at it, but the room's contents were emblazoned on the inside of her eyelids. A king-size bed piled high with dozens of pillows and a rose-colored comforter, so thick it appeared to add another layer to the box spring and mattress. The headboard was rosewood, carved with flowers in shapes that had never existed in the real world.

The bed might have been transported to this house from a fairy tale.

But it wasn't the bed that most fascinated Francesca. It was the bookshelves. They grew up, from floor to ceiling, on every wall in the room. There had to be dozens of them, all beautifully carved rosewood, and all completely overwhelmed with books.

Francesca had thought that her bookshelves were full, stuffed as they were with three or four layers of books, thrust every which way into any available space.

These bookshelves, though, they had taken the term *stuffed* and expanded it until the term could no longer contain the reality of the shelves and the books upon them. There had to be thousands of books in that room, piled every possible way upon those dozens of bookshelves, crammed in so tightly that removing one might cause an avalanche.

Francesca's fingers itched to get back in there and explore. She didn't know what kinds of books there were and she didn't care.

She reminded herself to check to see if one of the two other keys Marta had left her also worked on the inside doors. She would lock the room and put that key away until Joshua and Marta returned.

Paul led the way down the stairs.

"I'll make a pot of tea," she said, placing the book on the table. "Don't start until I get back."

CHAPTER 24

Francesca didn't know how to tell Paul that she wanted to read the book without him. In the end, she didn't have to. Paul looked at the clock behind the glass shelves and shook his head.

"I have to go. Are you going to be okay?" he asked, nodding toward the book on the table. "First lesson, tomorrow morning at nine. Make the coffee before I get here."

"Everything okay?" Francesca asked.

"Yeah, just time to go start dinner and then rush over to the hospital. Gotta run," he called, hurrying across the floor and out the door. "See you tomorrow," floated behind him as he left.

The kettle screeched as Francesca sat at the table, still weighing the book in her hands, still unwilling to open it.

"Tea," she muttered. "That's the answer."

Two hours later, she was still puttering around the shop, muttering to herself and avoiding the book like the plague. She had run upstairs, made her bed, checked out the titles on her bookshelf and spent some time staring out the window.

Next she went out to the garden. Francesca didn't know much about gardening, but she could water the plants and pull the obvious weeds.

She walked carefully along the brick paths, a large watering can she'd found on the back porch in hand. She looked for plants with drooping heads and watered them. She looked for dead flowers and plucked them. She touched the plants that tempted her, ones with furry leaves or soft-petaled blooms, and even tasted a few whose scents were astonishing—lemon and mint and pepper.

Working in the garden took her through until dinner.

And after dinner? She wanted to check behind the door at the top of the stairs. The door she hadn't opened.

The door matched the others, nothing unusual about it at all, and Francesca felt none of the discomfort she'd felt in opening Marta's door.

She swung it open and found nothing. A big empty nothing. Lace curtains to match hers on the windows, an open door into an empty closet, and another open door into a spotlessly clean and empty bathroom. Not even a dust bunny spoiled the perfect hardwood floors.

She wrinkled her brow. Now, this was odder than anything she'd seen yet. If this were her house…

Francesca shook her head, hard, and then bit the inside of her mouth.

"Not your house. Repeat after me. *Not your house*. Not ever going to be your house. You're short-term help. Unpaid help, at that. Not your house. Not your house."

Repeating the phrase, she went down and then back up the stairs, bringing the book and the tea with her. If she was going to read, she was going to be comfortable.

She took the extra pillows from the closet in her room, pulled a hand-knit throw from the linen closet in the bathroom, and settled back onto her bed, her tea and the book beside her.

She was as ready as she was ever going to be. The book was covered in faded and stained brown leather and it was thick, much thicker than any journal Francesca had seen. It smelled, not musty exactly, but old, as if it had been rained on, then left in the sun for too long.

Francesca had a pair of boots made of leather like that, boots she loved so much she had never been able to throw them away. She wore them on days when she needed to remember the good parts of her past. The days past when, occasionally, if she saved for three months, she had been able to splurge and buy a pair of *new* leather boots.

Now, though, no matter that she worked more hours, paid less rent, she still ended up with less money. And it wasn't because she spent more; in fact, she spent less than she had twenty years ago. The same amount of money just didn't go as far these days.

Francesca felt sorry for people who had a family. She couldn't imagine how they were managing. She barely made it, and she only had to feed one person. She didn't need a car to get to work; she didn't have fees or mortgages. She wasn't sick.

She brought her attention back to the book, stroking its patchy binding.

"Damn it, Francesca, just open the damn thing."

The first page was blank, the paper yellowed, the water stains from the cover seeped through to form the palest of brown blotches on the page.

She turned to the next. Letters faded away to nothing. Unreadable. Undecipherable.

The rain or damp had swallowed up the words, diluting the ink until it looked like the tide-soaked prints of the tiniest of shore birds. She could tell they'd been there; she couldn't decipher them.

Francesca frowned and turned to the next page. Still nothing she could read. The next was the same. Maybe, she thought, this wasn't going to be so hard after all.

Finally, though, ten or twelve pages in, part of a sentence appeared in the middle of the page.

...hair as red as flame...

And then nothing again.

Francesca continued to turn the pages, faster, catching glimpses of words and phrases and sentences. Twenty pages in, then thirty, the words began to follow her, wanting her to turn them into sentences.

Sorrow...

Lost my...

I thought he...

...and then the branch...

But now the words drifted slowly into sentences and then paragraphs.

Francesca put her finger in at the first full page and closed the book around it.

She took a deep breath, then another, then closed her eyes.

"I'm going to read this one story and then I'm going to put it down. That will be enough."

The few words she'd managed to read, the sorrow imbued in them, had spooked her and she was glad she hadn't taken Marta's advice to read the book at night.

Broad daylight was the best environment for this endeavor. She still needed to get some sleep and if these stories were all as sad as the phrases she'd gleaned from while flipping through those early pages, she was definitely going to need a walk in the sunlight before she got over them.

And there was always that bottle of Grand Marnier Paul had left behind. That would help, as well.

She snuggled into the pillows, enjoying the feel of the sun on her body. Her apartment got no direct sunlight, so chances like this were rare. She closed her eyes and drifted....

The red neon flashed and the heavy rain drowned out the sound of her footsteps. Francesca had slowed from her frantic run to a carefully silent skitter along the edges of the alley. They mustn't find her.

The gang members weren't very old, but they were big and mean. Francesca wasn't stupid; she was scared of these boys. She'd seen them get stopped and taken away in a police car a couple of weeks earlier, but now they were back on her block.

Up until that night, she had managed to avoid them, being careful to check out the block before she turned the corner, careful to leave the coffee shop at a time when she was pretty sure they were doing their business on some other block, not hers.

She had a pretty good idea what that business was and she'd called the police several times. They always showed up, she couldn't complain about that, but the gang members were smart. They never carried anything with them, stashing it somewhere the police couldn't find.

That night, though, she was unlucky. She left the Mouse and Icon later than usual, after filling in for Neo. She was so tired she hadn't done her usual reconnaissance before turning onto the street and she hadn't wanted to turn around and run once they'd noticed her.

She would have been better off running right then, while she had a half block lead. She'd remember that the next time. If she made it to the next time.

She had crossed the street to avoid them. It didn't work. They kept patrolling the street, looking for something or someone, and ended up in front of her building at almost the same moment as she did.

One of them watched her as she made her way down the block while the other two looked for… What? Victims? Customers? It didn't matter; they had Francesca in their sights even while they were looking for someone else.

She had tried to sneak behind them to get in the door, but the biggest one turned around when she kicked one of the many empty cans on the sidewalk.

"Hey, babe, wazzup?"

Francesca hung her head, her keys clasped tightly in her right hand, the pepper spray C.J. had forced on her in the left.

"It won't stop them," he'd said, "but it'll give you time to run. That's all you need. Promise me you'll carry it with you all the time."

She'd nodded at C.J., planning to keep the spray can in her bag.

"If it's dark, or you're somewhere you're not familiar with," he'd continued, "promise me you'll carry it in your hand. If you have to find it in that—" he glanced disgustedly at her big canvas bag "—it'll be too late."

She'd promised him and she kept her promise.

It was dark, she was scared, and she was carrying the pepper spray. She'd never had to use it, but Francesca's senses were tingling tonight. She grasped the can tighter and prepared herself for battle.

For a moment, she wished she'd never taken the extra shift; she wished she'd run as soon as she'd seen them on her block; she wished for C.J.

None of her wishes came true.

The three boys—she couldn't bring herself to call them men though they were as big as any men she knew, including C.J.—turned toward her, smiles on their faces.

The smiles weren't the slightest bit reassuring, more like a pack of wolves baring their teeth than friendly smiles.

Francesca ducked her head again and tried squeezing past them to the door.

They shuffled, just enough to get between her and the door, and then moved closer to her, crowding her away from the door and back onto the sidewalk.

"Excuse me," she said in a cracking voice. "That's my place right there."

"Is it?" the tallest man said. "What you got up there?"

"Nothing," she whispered.

"Duh," said one of the others, "this broad got nuthin'. She too old and too poor to have anything. She prolly got a kitty cat and a hot plate. That's it."

The three boys laughed and continued to crowd Francesca out onto the street.

C.J. would be disappointed if he'd trained the boys. They weren't watching her back, but all standing in front of her, leaving her an exit.

She raised the pepper spray in her trembling hand and pressed the button.

God, she thought, *I should have practiced. Nothing's happening*. She tried again.

A fine spray left the top of the pepper spray, coating her fingers, hitting the faces of the three men in front of her and wafting back into her eyes.

All four screamed, the boys much louder, and much angrier than her. The stream of pepper spray had hit them full in their faces.

Francesca backed off, ignoring the tears running from her eyes. She dropped the can and ran.

She bounced off a car, then fell to her knees when she tripped over a pothole. She swallowed the scream brought on by the pain, picked herself up and kept running.

She couldn't see through the tears and the dark more than a few feet in front of her. Her street, the streets in her neighborhood, had once had streetlights, but the boys and their friends liked to practice with slingshots on the bulbs, and the city had given up replacing them more than once or twice a year.

They'd been out of commission for almost six weeks this time. She hoped that her pursuers—for she heard them galloping behind her—were having as much trouble as she was seeing where they were going.

Francesca didn't care where she was going, didn't

keep track of the street signs or landmarks as she passed them. All she listened for was the slap, slap, slap of the feet behind her.

All she cared about was how close behind her they were.

She didn't dare look back.

She listened to their footsteps, thought they might be growing more distant, and let the rain wash the pain from her eyes.

Francesca ran.

She listened for the footsteps.

She ran some more.

She ran until the blisters on her feet made her hobble and then she hobbled until she got control of the pain.

Then she ran again until the blisters burst.

Blood from her knee flowed down to meet the blood on her feet. She ran.

She ran into an alley, soaked to the skin, her clothes clinging like seaweed to her back. Her feet were so sore she couldn't imagine taking another step without screaming.

She ran. She didn't scream, biting the noise off before it could leave her mouth.

She slowed as she entered the alley, her heart pounding, her chest heaving, trying to get enough breath into her lungs that she could breathe. *Just for a moment,* she thought, *I just want to breathe for a moment.*

Francesca sat bolt upright in the bed, sweat beading on her forehead and in the hollows formed by her body. She had managed to stop the scream before it left her mouth, but she could feel it, waiting in her throat for release.

The sun had fallen below the windows. Shadows filled the room, and Francesca reached over to flip on the lamp. As soft yellow light flooded the room; she felt the fear receding.

It was still with her—that specific fear had been since that night, but she had it under control now.

She lay back in the bed, careful not to close her eyes. She'd had the nightmare enough times to know that if she closed her eyes now, she would see their faces. They would be standing over her while she lay on the pavement waiting for the pain.

They used weapons. Knives. She'd seen them many times, their long shining blades used to intimidate, to frighten, to make a point.

She remembered mostly the big one, his face expressionless as he watched her on the sidewalk. But she'd remember all three of them.

Sometimes she woke up from the nightmare, just like that, standing in the alley, alone in the rain.

But more often, she woke and found herself lying in a puddle, the three boys standing over her, their knives shining in the red neon light.

She'd told no one the story. The police couldn't help; the neighbors too scared to do anything.

Francesca shivered and pulled the covers around her shoulders. She would go downstairs, make supper and bring it back up here.

She'd read Marta's book later.

CHAPTER 25

It was much later and Francesca was still avoiding Marta's book. She'd used every single one of the procrastination techniques she'd learned over the years.

She washed the kitchen floor, scrubbed down the countertops, polished the silverware, and washed the windows.

Her favorite procrastination technique—watching reality TV—wasn't possible without a TV, so she turned on the radio. It just wasn't the same.

She sat on the back porch, the brick of vanilla English toffee ice cream in her lap, and watched the bees travel from flower to flower, the birds hop around on the grass, the sun vanish behind the fence. It was almost as good as television.

But once the sun's long midsummer setting began, Francesca spent most of her time swatting at the mosquitoes and no-see-ums. Her options were rapidly diminishing.

Marta's book it was.

She checked the locks on the doors and windows. It wasn't that she expected anything to happen, because she didn't. Despite the episode with Paul Trevor and the police, she felt relatively safe in this house, on this street, but it wasn't her house. Whatever happened, she had to keep everything secure for Marta and Joshua.

Once everything was locked up, the stove checked and double-checked, the pot of tea and the bottle of Grand Marnier carried up to her room, Francesca settled in, but this time in the rocking chair, not on the bed.

She didn't want to fall asleep, not for a while yet. The tea steamed in a cup next to her and Marta's book had begun to feel familiar beneath her fingers.

Francesca found the page where the fading ended and the stories began, right in the middle of a sentence.

"...a mess," it began.

Francesca hesitated, unsure whether to read on about the mess. She'd heard Marta's story and knew just what those two words might entail.

She closed the book, but then opened it again and shrugged her shoulders. Maybe someone else's mess was exactly what she needed to make the boys' images vanish, to allow her to sleep through a night without waking in terror.

Or maybe, just maybe, she would use the book as a barrier to sleep. No television, no radio, just a book of other people's stories. Sad stories, she thought, thinking of Marta and remembering the sorrow she had occasionally glimpsed in Joshua's eyes.

And Francesca, flipping through the pages and catching a single word on this page, a short phrase on another, decided that these tragic stories might give her some perspective on her own life.

Because really, it wasn't that bad. She had friends. She had best friends. Susannah and C.J. had been there for her for so many years and in so many ways that she couldn't count them, couldn't even remember them all.

What she did remember, though, was the way Susannah and C.J. had seamlessly entered her life and the way they'd remained there, through thick and thin, sorrow and joy. They'd been at her side through richer and poorer—always poor, in her case—in sickness and in health. And she'd been there for them.

Tears welled in Francesca's eyes, but she blinked them away.

"I have been such an idiot," she whispered, holding Marta's book against her chest.

Susannah and C.J. were her friends forever.

She'd spent so much of her life scared of losing them, of asking too much, of fretting through every change in her circumstances. Or theirs.

Nothing would change what was between them. Nothing could change it. They were her family and family was forever.

Francesca sat in that room, the first room she'd felt at peace in since her father had died, and she thought about her mother.

The book could wait. She placed it, patting it tenderly as she did so, on the bookshelf next to the bed. She calculated the time change to Italy and then picked up the phone before she could stop herself. She dialed the number she had memorized years ago and never used. She waited, listening to the odd-sounding double ring with her fingers crossed. Because she wasn't sure she'd have the courage to dial it again.

She had no idea what she was going to say, but she knew it was time. Mystic Hearts had given her that. A female voice answered in Italian.

"Mom?"

"Frannie?"

"No one calls me that except you."

"And your father. He started calling you Frannie the day you were born."

"He did?"

"Hmm. He told me that he loved Italy almost as much as he loved me and he wanted his daughter to have a name as beautiful as she was sure to be, but the minute you were born he took to calling you Frannie."

Francesca settled back into the chair with a sigh, releasing a tension she hadn't realized she carried. She'd been carrying it for most of her life but now that it was gone she felt almost light-headed.

"Why?"

"He couldn't tell me. He just said to him you were Frannie. After a while, I started calling you that, too."

She paused for a minute while Francesca listened to the overseas dust on the line.

"Your father was very persuasive."

"I remember the year I didn't want to play softball. I think he talked about it every night for a month before I gave in."

"You broke your arm that year and he felt terrible. Swore to me he'd never try and talk you into any-thing again."

"He did, though, all the time. And every time he managed to convince me that I was wrong and he was right."

"He was like that, the best salesman I've ever met."

The two women sat at opposite ends of the world and remembered the man who'd brought them together and whose death had torn them apart.

A sob ripped from Francesca's throat.

"Mom?"

"It's okay, love. I understand, I do. And I don't blame you. I just… I couldn't deal with it, and I abandoned you. I'm so sorry."

"I'm sorry, too. As if it wasn't hard enough for you, anyway, I turned into a first-class bitch."

Francesca heard a hiccup from the phone, then a tiny giggle. She didn't think she'd heard her mother laugh since… Well, since before her father had died.

"I tell my friends," Francesca said, "that the hardest thing my mom ever did was not to kill me when I was a teenager. I tell them that I deserved it."

Her mom giggled again.

"We were both sad and neither of us knew how to deal with it or each other. I should have made us go to counseling," her mother said, "but I was scared of what I might find out. What if…?"

"What if what?"

"What if I found out that my daughter hated my guts? What if I found out she blamed me for her father's death? What if I found out I was to blame? I didn't think I could live with that."

"Oh, Mom." Francesca ignored the tears this time. "I blamed you because it was easier to do that than admit the truth. I wanted a reason, I wanted the world to make sense, so blaming you made it easy for me. Dad died for no reason at all. He was in the wrong place at the wrong time."

"But I sent him out for..."

"But you didn't run the red light."

Francesca listened to her mother's breath catching in her throat.

"Frannie? Are we okay now?"

"We are. Perfectly and completely and absolutely one hundred percent okay."

"I love you, Francesca Bond."

"I love you back, Mom."

Francesca held the phone to her ear for a long time after her mother had said, "Ciao," and promised to call back on Sunday night.

Funny how simple it was to solve a problem that had existed for almost as long as Francesca had been alive. Two words—*Mom* and *Frannie*—and everything that had come between them had fallen away.

Francesca had held on to her hurt and anger for so long that she felt empty without them, empty and scared.

She had imagined that, if she ever did make things up with her mother, she would get over being scared. But now she had another thing to be scared about. And because this new fear was so completely unfamiliar, Francesca had no idea what to do about it.

Her anger had kept her going all these years, pushed her right through the fear she lived with on a daily basis. Now, in one short telephone conversation, she had lost the anger. She hadn't planned that, not at all, but it was gone.

Francesca checked again. Yep, it was definitely gone. Not a single shred of anger remained. She checked her stomach. Free of the clenching. She checked her shoulders. Relaxed.

She stood up and moved over to the bathroom, turning on every light, including the heat lamp in the ceiling. She took a good look in the mirror. The vertical line that had taken up permanent residence between her eyebrows was gone and her face seemed softer.

Leaning her forehead against the mirror, Francesca breathed a tiny patch of mist onto the glass. "Damn," she breathed, "what am I going to do now?"

She took one more quick look in the mirror, scowling at the woman looking back at her. She didn't like what she saw.

"You're too soft," she growled, "too soft to make it in this world. It's a scary, scary place out there."

She paused. Scary, she thought, wasn't a big enough description to tell this new woman what Francesca Bond knew about the world outside this house.

"It's more than scary," she continued. "It's not safe. There are terrible people out there and they're just waiting for some little innocent, with a sweet little smile on her face and a pair of eyes as soft as a kitten's, to show up so they can blow her away."

She looked again. The woman in the mirror still looked relaxed.

"You don't get it, do you?"

She waggled her finger at the face in the mirror. It had always worked with her. Teachers were the best at it. Every time one of them had waggled their index finger in her face, Francesca had backed down. There was magic in that finger.

But it didn't work on the new and improved—or not—Francesca.

"Frannie," she groaned, thinking of her mother and the name from her childhood.

"OhmiGod, that's what's done it, isn't it? You're reverting to your childhood. Well, missy, you just better forget everything you remember about that safe life and get your butt in gear learning all about this new world you're living in. Sweetness and light don't cut it around here."

The mirror Frannie grinned back at Francesca and defied her orders.

"No, no, no. You just listen to me. The world out there—" Francesca swung her arm in a big circle "—will eat you up and spit you out. Let me tell you a story about that."

Francesca couldn't help herself—she burst into laughter, then turned away from the mirror. This conversation wasn't helping a bit. *Sleep,* she thought, looking at her watch, *what I really need is some sleep. Things will look different in the morning.*

She washed her face, eyes closed so she wouldn't have to see the woman in the mirror, then fumbled with the wall by the door, trying to find the light switch. She didn't want to see her other self, even by accident.

The soft glow from her bedside lamp beckoned. She fell onto the bed.

Francesca patted Marta's book, promising it, "Tomorrow," and picked up *The Keeper of the Bees*. But Marta's book drew her and, in the end, she reached for it instead of Gene Stratton-Porter.

Five hours later, her eyes itching from tears shed, her head aching, she hugged the worn leather binding to her chest and thought about Mystic Hearts and the people who had been helped over the years.

She thought about the fireman who'd become a priest; the woman who had abandoned her children for drugs and sex but had made a new life with them many years later; the teenager who had run away from an abusive parent and become a counselor; the half a dozen soldiers who had found surcease from their guilt and anger in this house.

She thought about Joshua and Marta, whose story was represented in the book with only a few words.

I, Marta Van Iperen, was saved from myself by Joshua Bains and Mystic Hearts.

But Francesca had learned more from Marta's book than stories of redemption. She had learned more, she thought, than Marta had intended her to. But she was sure Joshua would have anticipated her response to the book.

He had given his permission for her to read the stories. That had to mean something more than just helping her out with her bedtime reading.

No, Joshua meant Francesca to connect with Mystic Hearts. The heart attack must have scared him, of course, but it also must have worried him. What if he left the world without telling anyone what Mystic Hearts was? What Mystic Hearts was capable of?

She searched her room, looking at it with fresh

eyes. These two rooms at the top of the stairs, one empty, waiting for its occupant; her room, decorated as if she'd planned it herself, the glass cases, the red neon, even the candies and chocolate, all had a single goal. They were designed for comfort, for solace, for serenity. They were crafted with loving care to relax even the most angry or hurt souls.

Mystic Hearts had taught Joshua what was needed to save someone's life. Not all the stories began with a gun in someone's hand, but they all ended with a new life.

Francesca had seen Joshua's gradual awakening to the power of the house through the stories. In the beginning, she thought, he'd had no idea what was happening, but his heart was open to others who, like himself, had been through hell and were ready to take up permanent residence there.

He hadn't told Marta the stories in strict chronological order, or at least she hadn't written them down that way, but the time frames were obvious. Soldiers, mostly, or their sorrowing wives or children just after wars ended. Women filled with pain and self-doubt during times of economic hardship.

And Paul Trevor. Francesca recognized him in the words even before Marta used his name. She shook her head. Her reaction to Paul, made more intense by the knowledge contained in Marta's book, could wait for another day.

Because the book had taught her more than stories. The words combined with the myths about the House she'd heard in the coffee shop and the Mouse. Midsummer eve had always been full of the magic of transformation and Mystic Hearts held some of that magic.

Once again, she fell asleep as the gray light of dawn lit the windows, still clothed, light on and the book pressed against her cheek.

CHAPTER 26

Pounding at the front door ripped Francesca from sleep. The sun streaming through the windows finished the job.

"Wait," she yelled down the stairs. "I'll be right there."

She had no idea how long the pounding had been going on but she did know, glancing at her watch, that three hours of sleep was definitely not enough.

She pulled a brush through her hair, squirted a glop of toothpaste into her mouth and swished it around while she raced down to the store.

When she pulled up the blind on the door, she realized she wasn't the slightest bit surprised to see Paul Trevor standing on the stoop outside. She'd been thinking and dreaming about him so much that his presence seemed natural.

"Come on in, I'll put the coffee on."

She caught a flash of surprise on his face as he pushed past her into the kitchen.

"I'll get it. You look a bit tired this morning."

Francesca's hackles stirred at the implications of that comment, but she soothed them down. Sitting was about all she was capable of right now, and coffee, especially coffee she didn't have to make herself, sounded better than anger. Especially since Francesca's coffee-making skills were about on a par with her candy-making skills.

"Thanks," she bellowed, pitching her voice to be heard over the running water in the kitchen.

Soon the smell of coffee brewing wafted into the shop and Francesca's taste buds stirred. Despite all the sensations she'd lost working long hours and long years in coffee shops, the allure of coffee had remained. Just give her a whiff of that aroma, and she was like a hound on point, salivating and ready.

She drifted into a light sleep, her head resting on her arms on the table.

A warm hand touched the place where her shoulder met her neck.

"Francesca?"

A coffee cup waved under her nose.

"Coffee's ready. Wake up, little girl."

The coffee cup moved up, pulling Francesca's head with it. She refused to open her eyes, just holding out her hand for the cup and then lifting it to her mouth.

"Careful. It's hot."

"I don't care."

She pulled a deep breath of the coffee's rich aroma into her nostrils, and then settled her lips on the rim of the cup, and drank—all without opening her eyes.

She held out the empty cup.

"One more, please. And then I'll open my eyes."

A chuckle, and then footsteps moving away and back. A large hand cradled both of hers and placed a full cup between them.

"There you go. No rush. The cinnamon buns take a few minutes to thaw."

"Cinnamon buns?"

"I brought them over from my place. I wasn't sure whether you'd have anything to eat and Joshua wants to see you this morning."

Francesca finished the coffee and opened her eyes without commenting on Joshua's message. She didn't know what to make of it, or what to make of the fact that Paul, rather than Marta, delivered it.

Paul poured them both another cup, then sat down on the chair opposite, his back to the windows so only a silhouette was visible against the bright morning sun.

Somehow, seeing only an outline of Paul Trevor gave Francesca courage to say the things she knew she needed to say.

"I'm sorry about yesterday," she began. "I'm not very good about accepting help. Not from anyone. It's a hot-button thing for me. But I'm trying to figure out a way to deal with it."

"No worries. I used to be that way myself."

She fidgeted with the coffee cup while she worked up the courage to continue the conversation, if *conversation* it could be called.

"How did you get over it?"

"Joshua and this house set me on the path and then running Good Food completed the job."

Francesca lifted her eyebrows in a query.

"Hang on, I'm just going to grab the cinnamon buns from the oven. I don't want to burn them."

He spoke over his shoulder as he hurried into the kitchen.

"I make great cinnamon buns, just ask anyone."

The scent of cinnamon and warm sweet pastry and melting icing preceded Paul into the shop. Francesca smiled at the haphazard way the buns were piled up on the plate and the juggling Paul was doing with the buns, the pot of coffee, and two plates, complete with knives and forks.

"You don't need butter with these," he said, piling three buns onto his plate.

Francesca couldn't help it, she laughed at him. He was just like a teenage boy, pushing the pastries into his mouth and licking his sticky fingers. Just like a teenage boy…

Except watching him lick his fingers made her body tingle. She lowered her eyes so he wouldn't see her watching, wouldn't see the look she felt on her face. Emotion-burn coming up.

A sticky finger tugged on her chin, pulling it up until she looked him right in the eyes.

"Francesca?"

His breath, as sweet as the cinnamon buns, caressed her mouth. He leaned closer, touching her lips, lightly, with his.

"Francesca."

This time, the kiss lasted longer, hotter and more assertive, and Francesca responded. She raised her arms to his neck as he pulled her from the chair and tight up against him.

"Francesca." Her name a soft hum in his throat.

The exhaustion left her body in a whoosh of energy.

His hair wrapped itself around her fingers as she stroked the nape of his neck. Time vanished. Francesca wasn't sure whether a single moment or an eternity had passed while she'd been wrapped in Paul's embrace.

The phone shocked them out of it.

"Don't answer it," she whispered against his chest.

"I'm not going to. But I think you should."

Francesca reluctantly pulled herself out of his arms and headed for the phone.

Four rings. *Pick up, answering machine*. Nope.

Six rings. *Voice mail, where are you?* Nope.

Ten rings. She reached for the phone and added one more chore to her to-do list: *Get voice mail*.

"Yeah?" Francesca used her most annoyed voice.

"Francesca?"

"Marta. Sorry. I was busy."

"Tell Paul that he was supposed to be bringing you to the hospital this morning."

Francesca moved the phone away from her ear to soften the sound of Marta's cough.

"We'll be right there."

The trip to the hospital was made in comfortable silence. Francesca felt as if she had, with that single kiss, moved beyond any necessity to discuss it or their relationship. It was clear they had a relationship; it was serious; and, whatever it took to work it out, they'd do it.

Paul touched her hand as they pulled into the hospital parking lot.

"Are you okay?"

"I'm better than okay, but Joshua's waiting for us."

"He's not waiting for me, he's waiting for you. I

have to get back to work so I'll drop by the store later on tonight. I'm usually done by 9:00 or so."

Francesca waved and blew him a kiss as she hurried into the hospital. Joshua was waiting for her.

"Francesca?"

Joshua moderated his voice. Yesterday, he'd had to work almost as hard as Marta to be heard. He felt better, rested and slightly stronger, and that showed in his voice.

She sat next to his bed on the chair Marta had just vacated. He'd sent her down to the cafeteria to have something to eat, although he was sure she realized he'd done it so he could have some time alone with Francesca.

Joshua reached for her hand. It lay warm and soft in his chilled palm.

"You're cold. Let me get you another blanket."

She leaped up from the chair but he pulled her back down, shaking his head.

"My hands are always cold. Warm heart, you know."

She smiled and nodded. "I do know."

"You've read Marta's book?"

"All of it." Francesca pointed at her eyes. "See these bags? I think I had about three hours sleep last night."

"I need to talk to you about Mystic Hearts."

This time, Francesca's smile was less mischievous and more… Well, it was more something, Joshua thought, though he couldn't tell what it was more of. Peace, maybe, or serenity.

"You don't, you know. I felt it the first time I saw the house. And she spoke to me last night."

"She spoke to you?"

"Not really, but when I was reading the book, I felt her presence. She wants me there."

Francesca's face reddened as she spoke those words. Joshua wondered why, and then understood. It couldn't have been easy—Joshua laughed at the understatement—to come right out and say she belonged in someone else's home.

Whatever Joshua had planned to say to Francesca about Mystic Hearts flew right out of his head. The house had done his work for him.

"Marta and I want you there. We need you there."

Joshua wanted to go on, to tell Francesca that Mystic Hearts was hers, that he'd already had his lawyer come in and had already signed a will leaving the house to her.

Marta, as always, saved Joshua from himself. She stood in the door of the room shaking her head at him.

"No," she mouthed, "no more."

And then out loud she said, "I've brought you some coffee, Francesca. I know it's not as good as Paul's, I don't think anyone can make coffee like Paul Trevor, but at least it's hot and caffeinated."

Joshua watched while Marta calmed Francesca without speaking a word. She touched her shoulder, then handed her a cup of steaming rotten hospital coffee. She sat down on the edge of the bed, her knees touching Francesca's, and leaned toward her.

Marta started to hum, then stopped. Joshua watched as Francesca's shoulders tensed up again.

"Do you mind? Joshua's nurses seem to think that the music keeps his blood pressure down."

Francesca shook her head.

"Please. Don't stop."

Francesca curled her legs up under herself, rested her head on the back of the uncomfortable hospital chair and fell asleep to the sound of Marta's humming.

When she woke, she had forgotten where she was, starting out of the chair with a screech and a moan of pain. Her legs buckled under her. She grabbed the side of the bed and hung on, waiting while the pins and needles subsided in her legs.

She looked down at the bed. Joshua and Marta

were so soundly asleep that even Francesca's moan and her jostling of the bed hadn't managed to wake them.

They were too still. Francesca started to panic, her heart racing, her hands stiff as she reached out to touch the bodies. They were warm, she thought. Surely that was a good thing.

She double-checked, leaning close enough to hear Joshua's faint snort as he breathed in and Marta's whistle as she struggled to keep the air moving in and out of her damaged throat.

Francesca took a small notebook from her pocket. She'd taken to carrying it with her to write down the multitude of items she needed to add to her various to-do lists. The front page, her Mystic Hearts to-do list, bore only one item: *Get voice mail.*

She didn't need to talk to Joshua about that; in fact, she realized with a start, she didn't need to talk to Joshua about anything.

The house was her responsibility now and she would make whatever decisions were necessary. Oh, she'd consult with Joshua but it would only be a courtesy. She knew, without question, that Joshua would defer to her.

Francesca shivered. She touched the back of her hand to her forehead. Maybe she was running a fever?

Because Francesca had never, not for a single moment in her life, felt so sure of anything. But her forehead was cool, or at least it was the same temperature as her hand and that felt normal.

She searched her gut for the fear that had woven knots in her stomach even as recently as the drive to the hospital. Nothing. It was as if all her intestines had straightened themselves out while she'd slept, as if all the acid and the turmoil had flushed itself away while Marta had hummed.

Francesca shook herself all over, like Susannah's dog had done that long-ago summer. And then she settled down to check in with each of her symptoms.

Forehead? Dry and warm, but not too warm.

Neck and shoulders? Relaxed.

Teeth and jaw? Not clenched, but supple.

She held out her hands. They waited without a tremor for her to decide what to do with them.

Stomach? Already checked. Perfectly normal, at least as Francesca imagined normal. She was pretty sure she'd forgotten what normal felt like but there were no gurglings, no knife thrusts of pain, no knots.

Toes? She wiggled them, no involuntary twinges or muscle pain.

She had saved the most complicated symptom

for last. Because even if her body had given up the pursuit of fear, if her mind hadn't accepted its absence, the changes to her body—though welcome—would not be enough.

Francesca wasn't quite sure how to check her mind but she did her best. She slowed her breathing, closed her eyes, and waited. Normally, a few moments of complete silence and her mind would begin an endless round of fretting.

What if was its regular refrain.

What if Joshua and Marta don't want me?

What if Paul doesn't really care about me?

What if I lose both *my jobs and Mystic Hearts doesn't work out?*

What if I get cancer?

What if Joshua dies?

What if I end up as a bag lady?

What if?

None of those questions seemed to be waiting to jump out and start the downward spiral.

Francesca considered the small ones. Sometimes the process began with something quite innocuous like: *What if I forgot my keys?*

What if my blister bursts?

Francesca waited for the litany to begin. And waited. And waited.

For the first time in her grown-up life, Francesca's mind didn't start the sequence, not with the big questions nor with the small ones.

She tucked a note into Marta's hand.

I'll see you tomorrow, it said. *I'm going home, the garden needs watering*.

Francesca smiled to herself. She hadn't even felt a twinge of hesitation about writing the word *home*. Now that was progress.

CHAPTER 27

Joshua and Marta stayed at the hospital more than long enough for Francesca to learn how to make pastry under Paul's tutelage. She went through uncountable pounds of butter, thirty or forty pounds each of white and brown sugar, burned half a dozen muffin tins beyond recognition, and set afire an uneven number of oven mitts.

"You're a walking advertisement for aloe," Paul muttered, breaking off yet another branch and rubbing the soothing ointment over Francesca's finger. "The oven's hot," he said, rapping his knuckles on Francesca's forehead. "Hot."

Francesca giggled. She'd spent most of the lessons giggling. Learning to cook—in a hurry—from a temperamental prima donna army-trained pastry chef called for either a temperament to match, which Francesca didn't have, or an unceasing supply of laughter.

Francesca chose the latter.

She spent the mornings with Paul, learning to

feel rather than make pastry. Recipes were only a starting point for him; making pastry was all about touch.

"Feel this," he would say, pressing Francesca's hand into a mound of puff pastry or pie pastry or scone dough. "This is what it should feel like."

Weeks into her intensive education, Francesca still couldn't tell the difference between sweet dough and regular, couldn't *feel* when the pie crust was ready. But she wrote down everything Paul told her, measuring both by volume and weight, and watched his hands.

She watched his hands in the kitchen making pastry and thought about the way those hands, strong and warm and tender on her skin, might make her feel at night.

She spent the afternoons serving pastries, coffee and tea to the neighborhood regulars. Every day people came in and asked about Joshua and Marta and then ordered whatever Francesca had made that morning. They drank coffee, chatted with whoever sat at the table next to them, and smiled at Francesca, all the while ignoring the hammering in the back garden.

The children showed up around 3:30, pressing their little noses against the glass candy cases. The cases weren't as full or as lush as they had been before Joshua had gone to the hospital, and Paul was still making most of the contents, but Francesca's offerings were starting to show up on the shelves on a regular basis.

The noise in the back garden didn't bother Francesca a bit; in fact, she loved it. Paul and his clients were working on a project that Francesca and Paul had come up with once they'd realized that Joshua might get better, but he'd never be well again.

Paul had found the wood in the shed at the back of the garden, called in favors from plumbers and electricians and architects, even a few cops, and all of them—Paul, his clients, the unpaid volunteers—enjoyed every minute of the construction. The sounds of laughter and snatches of song filled the garden for those three hours every afternoon.

Her days were much of a muchness, a lovely, warm, settled kind of muchness. And the best day of all was the day Marta and Joshua got married.

"I didn't give him a choice," Marta whispered, standing beside the hospital bed holding Joshua's hand. "I told him he was marrying me or else."

Joshua smiled up at Marta so sweetly, Francesca had to turn away before the tears spilled from her eyes.

"Marta's or-elses are frightening," he said. "I had to say yes."

Father Henry grinned at all of them. “Okay,” he said, “let’s get on with the show.”

Francesca didn’t think she’d ever forget the look in their eyes as Father Henry pronounced them married. Love, hope and faith in the future tangled with a desire so strong it made Francesca’s knees shake just seeing it.

Francesca loved the days at Mystic Hearts, but she loved the nights even more.

She spent them with Paul, making candy. She did much better with those lessons. She burned herself just as much but she learned to make fudge, and divinity and macaroons. She shaped marzipan animals and licorice whips. She dipped cherries in milk chocolate and candied ginger in dark chocolate that Paul made without her. Making chocolate was one thing too many.

She spent them with Paul, making love. The smells of chocolate and orange and ginger permeated their skin, and she tasted it on his neck when she kissed him, on his hands when they touched her lips.

She learned how to touch him, learned to listen for the hitch in his breath when she touched his nipples or his belly. She learned to relax and enjoy each moment as he touched her. She learned to kiss him until neither of them could breathe.

The lessons she learned with Paul in the magical darkness of Mystic Hearts were the easiest lessons of her life.

They spent each night together, sliding from candy making to lovemaking to sleeping curled around each other without pause between.

The first night, as they'd tasted each other's bodies, Paul had stopped and lifted his head to watch her in the light from the candles.

"I never once believed I could have what Joshua and Marta have. Yet here you are."

He'd pulled her into his arms until they'd been so close she'd seen the tears in his eyes. She'd smiled and touched her tongue to them.

"Here we are," she'd said, "and your tears taste of orange and chocolate and love."

At dawn, when he left her, Francesca learned the pang of longing as he slid from her bed, and welcomed it. She learned the sweet aftermath of passion as she lay in her bed and waited for the birds in Marta's garden to wake her to another day.

And she learned to enjoy each day with only the slightest hint of fear, no longer the fear of anger or pain or despair, only the fear of loss.

In those weeks, learning to cook, learning to love, Francesca's life became all about touch and taste.

Her hands and arms told the story. She had burns coloring her skin like measles, from the tips of her fingers to her elbows. Even her tongue suffered.

She couldn't resist the taste of Paul. Or his cooking. She grabbed scones from the pan and bit into them, the cheese or raspberries bursting into pain on her tongue.

Early each morning, Paul stopped at the florist on his way over to pick up a new aloe plant because by nightfall the previous days' plant was decimated to soothe one more day's worth of burns.

Francesca learned to stay up late and sleep until just past dawn. It was the only way she could get all her lessons in.

Every evening after an early dinner, Paul finished up at Good Food, packed up a bag full of leftovers and another recipe, and arrived at Mystic Hearts just as the summer sun set.

He left each morning just early enough to get back to Good Food to make sure his clients were safely settled in.

One day, long into the lessons, Marta came by to drop off her dirty clothes and pick up some clean ones. She sat Francesca down in her favorite chair, brought her a cup of tea, sampled the scones, then the croissants and cinnamon buns and passed her.

"You don't get an A, or even a B, but I'll give you

a C minus. You make good enough pastry to serve at Bains Candies or feed that man of yours. Just make sure the coffee's strong," she suggested. "It'll disguise the flavor."

"I make good pastry, Marta. Maybe not Cordon Bleu pastry but I think it's pretty darn good. And so does Paul."

Marta sniggered, something six weeks ago Francesca couldn't have imagined her doing.

"I bet he does."

CHAPTER 28

Francesca hadn't told Marta and Joshua about Paul, but of course they knew. They probably knew the day they'd first kissed; knew the night they'd made love for the first time. She didn't think Marta had said anything to Paul, though Francesca had caught her watching the two of them together.

Paul didn't need to marry her, didn't need her to move in with him. He didn't want her to give up her life's work now that she'd finally found it, and wasn't willing to give up his. They'd crafted a life together that worked, that brought them joy.

"Vacations," she said one night, her hands tangled in his hair. "We'll take vacations together so we can wake up in the same bed, so we can make love in the mornings and not just at night."

"Hmm," he said, "I like the way you think. When can we take the first one?"

"I like the way he treats you," Marta said. "He's good to you, Francesca. When are you getting married?"

"We're not getting married."

"You've talked about it?" Marta raised her eyebrows.

"Yes, of course we've talked about it. Weeks ago."

Francesca smiled as she thought of *that* conversation and where it had led.

Late-afternoon sunlight had sparkled on the bed in her room, lighting up the hairs on Paul's chest, the ones that were tickling her nose.

"Francesca? What do you think about marriage?"

"Is this a proposal or a rhetorical question?"

"A little of both, I guess."

Francesca had rolled over to face him.

"If I was going to marry anyone," Francesca had said, smiling and running her fingers over his lips, "it would be you."

"Me, too. But…?"

"I can't leave Mystic Hearts. You can't leave Good Food. Things are good…."

He placed a finger on her lips, interrupting her.

"They're better than good, they're great. They're perfect. You're perfect."

"We're perfect, so why spoil it?"

"So you're not getting married?" Marta prodded. She could never let things go.

"Nope."

"And you're okay with that?"

Marta's eyebrows quirked down at the outside edges and the lines on her forehead became pronounced. Francesca knew she wasn't happy with the answer but she didn't have another one.

She tried to explain.

"We don't need to get married. Everything's good just the way it is. I finally have a job and a home I love, and Paul does, too. And we have each other."

Marta shrugged and left it.

A week later, she fretted at the front door of the hospital. She was waiting for Paul to pick them up, but she knew Joshua wasn't ready to go back to Mystic Hearts. It didn't matter that the doctors had insisted it was time for him to go home.

She'd watched him walk painfully from the bed to the bathroom and back. She'd seen the strain on his face, the way he cringed each time he rolled over in bed. It had taken them almost two months in the hospital to stabilize him and he still had trouble getting around.

Paul hurried through the door and over to her.

"Ready?"

Marta nodded. She had no energy today to waste on talking, no breath for it. She needed it all to get Joshua home, giving everything she had to him, humming because it seemed to soothe the pain, keeping her hand on his chest because it seemed to relax him enough to sleep.

"Where's Joshua?"

Marta pointed at the nurses' station.

"I'll go get him?"

She nodded again.

Paul had seen Joshua almost every day since he'd been in the hospital. He'd charted his progress—or lack of it—but seeing him this day still shocked him.

Joshua sat in a wheelchair at the nurses' station, women in nurses' uniforms and doctors' lab coats gathered around him. His face was gray with pain, and he had progressed far past thin into gaunt. Each bone in his body showed, even through his clothing.

And his face? Paul wanted to weep when he looked at Joshua's face.

But when Joshua looked up and smiled at him, Paul saw only joy in Joshua's eyes. And acceptance.

He wasn't going back to Bains Candies to take over from Francesca; he was going home to Mystic Hearts to die. He might have another year, or two, but he knew and had accepted what was coming.

Paul bundled Joshua and Marta into the truck. Marta's humming took away the chill he'd been feeling since he had seen Joshua's smile. Maybe it wasn't going to happen today, or even tomorrow. Maybe Joshua and Marta could have enough time together for Marta to figure out how she was going to live without him.

And maybe, just maybe, Paul would be able to figure out the same thing.

Francesca had to be the one to help her do that. She had learned so much from Marta.

When the two of them were together, the world became tranquil. And warm. As if the perfect midsummer day followed them, turning the world around them into the soft hum of a July day.

Francesca had been transformed over the past months.

He wanted it be about him, but he knew he was only a small part of it. Joshua and Marta and Mystic Hearts had all worked their magic on her.

The fear so often clouding her eyes had vanished. She spent her days laughing and crying with equal abandon, never once hiding her emotions.

If she was angry, and Paul often made her angry, she showed it without hesitation and without any holding back.

"You idiot," she'd say and smack his hand away from the oven, "you told me to use shortening. And now look what you've made me do."

And she'd pull a pie from the oven, the crust burned and dry. "Your fault," she'd cry, dropping the pie to the floor. "You clean it up." And she'd storm from the kitchen into the garden.

She would come home from the hospital and walk out the back and straight into Paul's arms, the tears streaming down her face.

"He's worse," she'd say. "Marta doesn't see it. She thinks he's going to be fine."

Paul would nod and say, "Yes, I know," and they'd cling to each other until the tears were all cried out.

"He's coming home, though, isn't he?" she'd ask each day, and Paul could say only, "I hope so," and continue on with his work.

Paul couldn't help but smile when he thought of what he'd gained over the past months.

Francesca.

He didn't know how to describe how he felt about Francesca but it was something he'd never felt before. He hadn't even been able to imagine her; she was completely beyond his imagination. She was the woman he would have wanted if he'd known enough to want a perfect life.

Vacations. He spent most of his days thinking of vacations, planning trips to take with Francesca.

He brought his mind back to the job at hand.

"Why the alley?" Joshua asked, as Paul turned into the tree-lined alley backing onto Mystic Hearts.

Paul smiled through the windscreen at Francesca waiting at the gate.

"You'll see."

Paul lifted Joshua into his arms and carried him to the back gate. Francesca wrapped her arm around Marta's shoulder and pulled her after them.

When Paul reached the gate, Francesca hauled it open and stepped back with a flourish.

The tiny house they'd spent the past six weeks building for Joshua and Marta glowed. The garden was at its best and Francesca had planted even more flowers around the new house. She'd planted every flower she could find, even some she'd had to order from a nursery over the Internet.

Eglantine and musk-roses.

Woodbine and oxlips.

Violets and wild thyme.

No one but her would know what they meant, but Francesca, unlike Joshua, believed in the magic of a midsummer night. It had changed her life after all.

The house Paul and his clients and friends had built was a miniature of Mystic Hearts, right down to the gables and the shutters.

A gently sloping ramp led up to the front door and Paul carried Joshua right up and into the big main room.

The furniture from their second-floor room had been rearranged into the new house and looked as if it belonged there.

Paul settled Joshua into his big leather chair and Joshua smiled, then reached out his hand for Marta.

"We're home, my angel, my beautiful one. This is the new Mystic Hearts.

"Thank you, both of you. You could not have done anything I, we—" he held up their joined hands "—would have liked better."

CHAPTER 29

Midsummer eve, midnight

Rain. And red neon. Francesca stood at the window of Bains Candies looking out at the alley, the one that hadn't been there five minutes earlier. The thin streams of rain turned crimson, lighting the alley like a horror film.

She had asked Paul to stay home this night, had asked Joshua and Marta to let her do this alone. She promised all three she would call if she needed help. Francesca crossed her fingers. She wanted to do this on her own.

She'd been standing at the window for most of the evening. She had wanted to see the alley appear, wanted to see the red neon start flashing. Because she still didn't believe it was possible. What she had seen last year had to have been her imagination.

She had crawled all over Mystic Hearts since it

had become her home. She had checked every electrical connection, climbed over each inch of the steep gabled roof, used ladders to inspect every window frame from both the inside and the outside. There was no evidence of a neon sign, and no dark inner-city alley anywhere in sight.

The light came from somewhere over her head. She ran upstairs, looked out each window, but the flashing came from above her. She pulled down the ladder to the attic, grabbed the flashlight she'd taped to the steps and went up. No sign. The neon flashing still came from above her head.

Back in her room, she stuck her head out the window and peered up through the rain trying to see the source of the red light. Soaked through, she gave it up and headed back downstairs to wait by the door.

Joshua hadn't explained this part of Mystic Hearts—how it changed location, how the sign appeared, how it called people to her—to Francesca, mostly because she'd been too scared to ask. And now she thought it might have been that he didn't understand it any more or any better than she did.

The mystic side of the house was already way over her head, and she hadn't been able to convince herself that she hadn't imagined the dark alley and the flashing neon. So she hadn't asked.

Yet here they were.

The empty room at the top of the stairs was empty no longer. Francesca had ordered a new bed, covered it with dark sheets and soft pillows. She'd filled the bookcase with boys' stories of adventure. *Treasure Island*, *Lord of the Rings*, Rudyard Kipling, Harry Potter and *The Hitchhiker's Guide to the Galaxy*.

She'd put a razor and unscented shaving cream in the bathroom along with the dark green towels and an extra-large matching robe. The drawers of the dresser contained cedar chips and black T-shirts and jeans.

The pictures? She'd ended up with Japanese woodblocks of the ocean and Mount Fuji and prints that reminded her of Middle Earth.

Francesca had avoided thinking too carefully about what she was doing and who the house might be expecting. It felt right so she did it. The house had taught her that.

But she still wasn't ready. She might never be ready. She glanced at her watch and shivered.

And there, right on time, was the shadow at the door. Goose bumps ran up and down her arms, merging with the hair standing straight up on her neck. Gulp. Double gulp.

Francesca wanted to run out the back door and

get Joshua. She wanted to go back to her one-room apartment and her other life. She wanted to… Mostly, she thought, she wanted to panic.

Her heart pounded in her chest. Panic, sign one. Her face heated up. Panic, sign two. Her mouth and her lips dried out. Panic, sign three. And she started to shake. Panic, sign four.

Okay, she no longer *wanted* to panic, she *was* panicking. Now what? Joshua?

No, Joshua wasn't the answer. He was getting frailer by the day. It was a miracle he'd lived through the year, but he was hanging on. She would have to figure this out on her own.

Step one. Go to the door. She peeked out around the sign but saw only the back of a tall shadow, male, she thought, dressed in black and dripping wet. Hoodie pulled forward over his face, baggy pants, and everything clinging to him with rain.

Step two. Open the door.

"I can't," Francesca whispered. "I can't do it."

She rested her head against the door, the glass cool and damp against her cheek.

"Take a deep breath."

She did.

The panic didn't disappear but it did slow to code yellow, allowing her to breathe and her heart to stop banging against her rib cage.

She lifted her head and looked out the window directly into the eyes of her nightmare. He had been there that night, chased her through the streets, though he hadn't been the ringleader.

They watched each other through the glass, the red neon blinking. On. She saw his face, looking as scared as she felt. Off. A shadow. On. His face limned in red. Off. A shadow again.

She wasn't sure which of them blinked first. She backed away from the door, scrambling backward like a crab surprised out from under a rock on the beach.

He knocked on the glass. "Miss?" He held up a shaking hand coated in blood. "Can you help me?"

He fell to his knees on the stoop. "Miss?"

She threw caution out with her panic and flung open the door. She reached for his shoulder.

"Come in," she said, guiding him to her favorite table and pushing him down onto her chair. "Let me get you a towel."

She handed him the towel she'd placed ready on the radiator. She took another and wrapped it around the cut on his arm. The cotton felt warm and soft in her shaking hands.

"I'll make you some hot chocolate and then I'll call…"

"Not the ambulance." His voice shook and tears welled up in his eyes.

"I'll get the first-aid kit, instead. Okay?"

He nodded.

"Do you like marshmallows?" Francesca asked.

The face she'd found so frightening last year now lit up with a child's joy.

"I love marshmallows," he said. "They remind me of my mother."

The iron tongue of midnight hath told twelve:
Lovers to bed; 'tis almost fairy time.
—Shakespeare, *A Midsummer Night's Dream*